P9-AOY-479

TALL, DARK AND SEXY
The men who never fail—seduction included!

Brooding, successful and arrogant, these
men have a dangerous glint in their eye and
can sweep any female they desire off her
feet. But now there's only one woman each
man wants—and each will use their wealth,
power, charm and irresistibly seductive
ways to claim her!

Don't miss any of the titles in
this exciting collection:

The Billionaire's Virgin Bride
Helen Brooks

His Mistress by Marriage
Lee Wilkinson

The British Billionaire Affair
Susanne James

The Millionaire's Marriage Revenge
Amanda Browning

HELEN BROOKS was born and educated in Northampton, England. She met her husband at the age of sixteen and thirty-five years later the magic is still there. They have three lovely children and a menagerie of animals in the house! The children, friends and pets all keep the house buzzing and the food cupboards empty, but Helen wouldn't have it any other way.

Helen began writing in 1990 as she approached that milestone of a birthday—forty! She realized her two teenage ambitions (writing a novel and learning to drive) had been lost amid babies and family life, so she set about resurrecting them. Her first novel was accepted after one rewrite, and she passed her driving test (the former was a joy and the latter an unmitigated nightmare).

Being a committed Christian and fervent animal lover, Helen finds time is always at a premium. But she makes sure to fit in walks in the countryside with her husband and dogs, meals out followed by the cinema or theater, reading, swimming and visiting with friends. She also enjoys sitting in her wonderfully therapeutic, rambling old garden in the sun with a glass of red wine (under the guise of resting while thinking, of course!).

Since becoming a full-time writer, Helen has found her occupation to be one of pure joy. She loves exploring what makes people tick and finds the old adage "truth is stranger than fiction" to be absolutely true. She would love to hear from any readers, care of Harlequin Presents.

THE BILLIONAIRE'S VIRGIN BRIDE

HELEN BROOKS

~ TALL, DARK AND SEXY ~

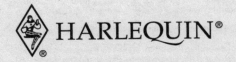

HARLEQUIN®

TORONTO • NEW YORK • LONDON
AMSTERDAM • PARIS • SYDNEY • HAMBURG
STOCKHOLM • ATHENS • TOKYO • MILAN • MADRID
PRAGUE • WARSAW • BUDAPEST • AUCKLAND

If you purchased this book without a cover you should be aware that this book is stolen property. It was reported as "unsold and destroyed" to the publisher, and neither the author nor the publisher has received any payment for this "stripped book."

ISBN-13: 978-0-373-82349-9
ISBN-10:   0-373-82349-5

THE BILLIONAIRE'S VIRGIN BRIDE

First North American Publication 2008.

Previously published in the U.K. under the title
A RUTHLESS AGREEMENT.

Copyright © 2005 by Helen Brooks.

All rights reserved. Except for use in any review, the reproduction or utilization of this work in whole or in part in any form by any electronic, mechanical or other means, now known or hereafter invented, including xerography, photocopying and recording, or in any information storage or retrieval system, is forbidden without the written permission of the publisher, Harlequin Enterprises Limited, 225 Duncan Mill Road, Don Mills, Ontario, Canada M3B 3K9.

This is a work of fiction. Names, characters, places and incidents are either the product of the author's imagination or are used fictitiously, and any resemblance to actual persons, living or dead, business establishments, events or locales is entirely coincidental.

This edition published by arrangement with Harlequin Books S.A.

® and TM are trademarks of the publisher. Trademarks indicated with ® are registered in the United States Patent and Trademark Office, the Canadian Trade Marks Office and in other countries.

www.eHarlequin.com

Printed in U.S.A.

THE BILLIONAIRE'S VIRGIN BRIDE

CHAPTER ONE

AM I doing the right thing? And if I am, why doesn't it feel like it? Why do I feel as though I'm teetering on the edge of a precipice?

The questions whirled in her head as they'd been doing for the last twenty-four hours, but outwardly the façade held. Anyone surveying her would see Melody Taylor, cool and collected as always and certainly not the type of woman to panic.

You asked him here because he's the best lawyer there is and that's what your mother needs right now. Personal issues don't feature in this so get a grip.

The self-admonition was sharp and brought her full mouth tightening in determination as her thoughts sped on.

You're going to show him that you're managing just fine without him, OK? It's easy as long as you don't lose your nerve. You handle difficult situations every day and you can handle Zeke Russell too.

The sitting-room door opened and her mother walked in, cutting short Melody's reverie. The look on the older woman's pale face brought Melody hurrying to her, her voice soft but firm when she said, 'Don't look like that; it'll be all right. I promise.'

'You don't know that, Melody.'

'Yes, I do, and you've got to believe it too. It's half the battle with something like this.'

'Oh, darling.' Anna Taylor touched her lips to her daughter's cheek in a fleeting kiss. 'What would I do without you?'

The endearment revealed the extent of her mother's distress. Melody had always known her mother loved her but Anna never demonstrated this physically or verbally except on the rarest of occasions.

The two women looked at each other for a moment and then Anna said, 'I don't like you having to ask a favour of Zeke either, not after everything that has happened.'

'I'm not asking him for a favour. We'll explain the situation and if he thinks he can take the case we'll pay him like any other client.'

'You know what I mean.'

Yes, she knew what her mother meant. And if she was being truthful she'd have to admit that if there had been any other way out of this than contacting Zeke she'd have taken it. But there wasn't. As a lawyer he was second to none and he won cases that appeared hopeless to everyone else. Those were the facts, unpalatable as they might be.

Melody shrugged. 'He agreed to come here so at least we don't have to go to his offices,' she said shortly. She didn't add 'and see Angela', but it was in both women's minds. Angela Brown was Zeke's sexy secretary and mistress—if their affair was still continuing. Melody ruthlessly put the thought of the other woman out of her mind. She had enough to concentrate on with Zeke arriving any minute.

The ring of the doorbell caused them both to freeze for a second, then Melody pulled herself together. 'That must be him now,' she said calmly, as though her heart wasn't trying to escape from her chest. 'Why don't you go and put the coffee pot on while I let him in?'

Another imperious ring made her soft, full mouth tighten. Forceful, determined, arrogant—Zeke obviously hadn't changed in the six months since they had last seen each other, not that she'd expected otherwise.

Her mother having fled to the temporary sanctuary of the kitchen, Melody walked out into the hall, taking a deep breath and composing her face into a polite smile before she opened the front door. She felt her eyes widen but hoped the tall dark man standing on the doorstep hadn't noticed. In spite of the way she'd tried to prepare herself for this moment all morning, the sight of him still took her breath away.

'Hello, Melody,' the deep, masculine voice murmured. There was only a faint trace of the American accent which proclaimed his early origins. 'How are you?'

'I'm f-fine.' She heard the slight stammer with an annoyance which provided a healthy shot of adrenaline. Her voice her own again, she continued, 'And yourself?'

'Wondering what your mysterious phone call is all about.' His head tilted slightly in the characteristic gesture she remembered when the razor-sharp brain was trying to make sense of something. 'I gather Anna's in some kind of trouble?'

Melody nodded. 'Do come in,' she said courteously, trying to ignore how very overpowering his presence was. At six feet four, Zeke was taller than most men and broad with it. She knew from experience there wasn't an ounce of fat on the massive frame, however; it was sheer muscled strength which padded his shoulders and chest. His face, with its sharply defined planes and angles, was attractive rather than handsome, the overall impression of hard cynicism etched into each feature. But his eyes... His eyes had always had the power to make her weak at the knees. A curious golden-amber colour, with thick, coal-black lashes which matched his close-cropped hair, they had the ability to hold an onlooker captive with seemingly little effort, an attribute he used to devastating effect with hostile witnesses in the courtroom.

The thought lingered as he strode past her into the hall, whereupon she shut the door and turned to face him again. By the end of their relationship, when everything which had been so right was so wrong, she had felt just like one of those poor unfortunates, she thought wryly. And it had been then she'd really understood why he was considered such a brilliant and formidable lawyer in spite of being a relatively young thirty-five years of age.

He waited for her to lead the way into the sitting room and she was careful not to brush against him as she passed. Nevertheless she couldn't help catching the faintest whiff of the delicious aftershave he used and her stomach muscles contracted and tightened as her heart galloped for a moment.

Steady, girl, steady, she warned herself silently as he followed her into the wide, pleasant room. This is a man who is an expert in reading people's faces to discover what they're thinking. You know that. Don't give anything away or you'll live to regret it. She turned, her voice civil and her eyes devoid of emotion. 'Sit down, Zeke. Mother's bringing the coffee through in a moment.'

The words hadn't left her lips before her mother appeared in the doorway, a large coffee tray in her hands. Melody moved to help her but Zeke got there first, taking the tray out of Anna's hands as he said quietly, 'Allow me. You're looking well, Anna.'

'Thank you.' Anna had adopted the role of hostess, her earlier distress hidden. 'So are you.'

Zeke Russell placed the tray on the long beech coffee-table in the middle of the room before straightening and surveying the two women. Still as alike as two peas in a pod, he thought in the moment of silence which ensued. You only had to look at Anna to see what Melody would look like in twenty years' time. Even at fifty, Anna was still quite dramatically lovely, her blonde hair shiny and sleek in an expertly cut bob and her skin showing little signs of ageing except round the eyes. Tall, slender and finely boned, the two of them could have passed for sisters rather than mother and daughter, albeit Anna seeming a somewhat older sibling. Of course their eyes were different, Anna's being a light blue which could be chilling on occasion, certainly when they focused on him. Melody's, on the other hand, were a warm, smoky grey with passionate undertones…

His body hardened but his voice was mild when he said, 'So, how can I help?'

It seemed to bring the two of them to life.

Melody pushed her mother down into a chair as she said, 'I'll see to the coffee, you explain what's happened.' And then, when Anna seemed incapable of beginning, Melody said, 'It's the business,' looking straight at him as she motioned for him to seat himself in a chair opposite her mother. 'You remember Julian Harper, Mother's personal assistant?'

Zeke nodded. Of course he remembered Anna's lapdog. He didn't think he'd ever met such an obsequious little toad as the small, greasy-haired individual who prided himself on being at Anna's beck and call, but whenever he'd made his feelings known in the past

Melody had defended the man to the hilt. Julian was devoted to her mother, she'd protested. Absolutely devoted. Her right-hand man in the business and a good friend too.

Zeke raised his eyebrows when it appeared Melody found it difficult to continue. 'Julian?' he prompted quietly.

'He's been fiddling the books.' It was Anna who cut in and her voice was steely now. Zeke recalled the tone. She had rarely spoken to him in any other way.

He turned his gaze to Melody's mother but she was looking somewhere over his left shoulder and wouldn't meet his eyes.

'Along with other dubious business practices,' she added bitterly. 'False orders, altering advice notes, inferior material…' She took a deep breath. 'And he's been clever too, making it look as though I was in on everything.'

'How?' Zeke had sat up straighter, his face suddenly intent. 'Forging your signature?'

'Nothing so obvious as that. I…I *have* signed things apparently that I shouldn't have. He'd bring a batch of papers for my signature and if I was busy…' Her voice trailed away before she added, 'I'd just sign them.'

Zeke looked at her with very real astonishment. He privately considered Anna Taylor to be one of the hardest women he had ever come across, a beautiful ice queen with a heart as frozen as the North Pole. He disliked her intensely and he knew the feeling was fully reciprocated. If someone had told him Melody's mother would ever sign a paper without reading it first he would have laughed them out of court.

She glanced at him and he knew she was fully aware of the nature of his thoughts.

Melody broke the contact by passing him a cup of coffee.

It was black and strong, exactly how he liked it, but then if his former fiancée didn't know his preferences, who would?

Their hands touched for the briefest of moments before Melody jerked hers away so abruptly the coffee was in danger of landing in his lap for a moment. A dart of dark satisfaction followed. So, not quite so together as she would like him to believe?

Zeke stretched his long legs, taking a pull at the coffee before he drawled, 'Do I gather this is in the public arena in some way?' as he glanced at Anna again.

The older woman inclined her head in confirmation. 'One of my main customers is claiming substandard material we supplied cost them hundreds of thousands,' she said flatly. 'Which I'm sure it did. It was a special order for a new line in lounge suites they were promoting. Within a matter of months the material was giving out and they had irate purchasers screaming the odds. They had to recall all the furniture, of course, but their reputation suffered as a result. When it first came to light I offered monetary recompense but they're looking for blood and intend to take me through the courts.'

Zeke nodded. He could have said it couldn't have happened to a nicer person in his opinion, but he didn't. Nevertheless he had to admit to a certain gratification that Anna was in this position. If it wasn't for Melody's mother's persistent manoeuvring and interference he and her daughter would be married by now, but Anna had plotted and schemed to split them up from day one. Of course, she couldn't have succeeded in her vendetta against him if Melody hadn't allowed her to.

His mouth hardened. 'Doesn't look too good for you, Anna, does it?' he murmured softly.

'I know that!'

The words were snapped out and Zeke saw Melody send her mother an anguished glance which said all too clearly, Don't lose your temper; be nice. Remember what's at stake.

And what was at stake? Anna's precious textile business. The business she had started twelve months after Melody's father had walked out on the pair of them when Melody was just three years old. He thought Melody's father needed a medal for staying that long!

Melody spoke now, her voice rushed as she said, 'Zeke, this is all so unfair. Mother could lose everything just because she trusted Julian. You do believe she didn't have anything to do with it?'

He allowed his eyes to rest on her face. It was flushed, her eyes deeply troubled and dark with emotion. She looked so lovely his guts twisted. He waited just long enough for his reply to carry a thread of insincerity when he said, 'Of course.'

'I knew this was a mistake.'

Anna spat the words, but when she went to rise to her feet Melody's voice was sharper than he'd ever heard it. 'Sit down, Mother, and don't be so stupid. You need Zeke far more than he needs you.'

He was surprised for the second time in as many minutes. In all the six months he and Melody had been together before she'd broken their week-old engagement and ended the relationship, he'd never heard her raise her voice to her mother. In fact he'd often wondered how she'd resisted Anna's demands that she come into the business when she'd left university. But it appeared that was the one time she hadn't indulged her mother, instead following her own star and becoming a speech therapist. He had met her when she had liaised with a partially deaf client he was defending.

Melody's gaze left her mother and centred on Zeke's expressionless face. She knew what that impassive look meant. He was thinking furiously behind the blank mask. She took a deep breath and attempted to sound matter-of-fact when she said, 'Like I said, Mother could lose everything if this goes against her. Regardless of whether you believe she's innocent or not, will you take the case and defend her?'

He stared at her without responding for a moment or two, then his voice was equally matter-of-fact when he spoke. 'I don't defend anyone I think is guilty, not unless there are extenuating circumstances, anyway.'

Melody swallowed against the tightness in her throat, hoping her mother wouldn't jump in again. 'Is that a yes or a no?'

In answer he turned and looked at Anna. 'Do you want me to defend you?' he asked quietly. 'It's clear what Melody wants, but how do you really feel? Do you want me as your lawyer?'

The silence stretched. At last Anna said, 'Yes.'

'Why?'

'Because I agree with Melody that you are the best in your field and I don't want to suffer for something I didn't do. I am innocent of these charges and if anyone can bring the truth to light I think you can.'

The silence descended again, heavier this time. Zeke stirred slightly. 'Are you aware you've given the one answer that would persuade me to take the case?' he asked drily.

Just as drily, Anna said, 'Of course.'

It was half an hour later when Melody saw Zeke out to his car, a flamboyant sports job parked on the small square of concrete which served as her mother's front garden. His briefcase was bulging with the papers Anna had presented to him, but Zeke had asked for others which they'd agreed would be delivered the next morning to his office in Kensington.

The May day was calm and warm, blossom stirring ever so gently on the trees bordering the street beyond the house and a little army of sparrows twittering high in the branches. Melody stood on the step of her mother's three-bed semi in Beckenham in greater London as Zeke walked to the car. The sunlight high-lighted the touch of grey in the black hair but it only added to the overall attractiveness of him as he turned to look at her.

'Make sure your mother understands I don't want her discussing this with anyone from this point on,' he said quietly. 'Should Julian come crawling out of his hole she says nothing, OK?'

Melody nodded. Julian had conveniently declared himself ill with nerves the day his deception had come to light, a doctor's letter arriving through the post the next day which stated the patient was suffering some form of a nervous breakdown due to overwork. Anna hadn't seen hide or hair of him since.

'Do you think you can win the case?' Melody asked flatly, her even tone not quite disguising her anxiety.

Zeke stared at her for a moment and then walked back to her. Melody nervously moistened her lips. Even though she was standing on the step and Zeke on the ground below, he seemed to tower over her.

'I always win,' he said softly. There was a pause and then he added, 'Except with you.'

Her heart beat harder. She'd known Zeke would bring

the matter of their broken engagement up sooner or later. 'That's in the past.' She attempted to sound casual.

'The hell it is.'

'This isn't about us.'

'Wrong.' The beautiful amber eyes held hers. 'Very wrong.'

'Zeke, it's been six months. I've moved on, *you've* moved on.' She heard the shakiness in her voice and could have kicked herself. This wasn't how you dealt with someone like Zeke Russell. Trembling softness wasn't an option.

'I agree—to a point. But there's unfinished business between us too. Maybe that's why you're still not dating?'

'How do you know I'm not seeing someone?' she asked hotly, prodding herself into angry retaliation to quell the hunger seeing him again had induced.

He didn't answer her, continuing to stare at her with the tawny gaze reminiscent of one of the big cats.

Something in his stillness made her take a step backwards into the hall as awareness hit. 'You've been spying on me,' she said, amazement warring with outrage. 'You have, haven't you?'

He didn't bother to deny it. 'Hardly spying,' he said lazily. 'Just making sure you didn't do something silly in the aftermath of the break-up.'

'Why should you care?' A thought hit her. 'Unless you imagined my seeing someone else would reflect badly on you? A girl has to take some time to get over Zeke Russell. Is that it?'

'Exactly.' And he had the audacity to smile.

Melody counted to ten. Her mother needed him to take the case. She had to remember that. 'And how's Angela?' she asked sweetly. 'Still your secretary I imagine?'

'You imagine right.' He looked her straight in the eye, his golden gaze inscrutable. 'She's damn good at what she does.'

'I don't doubt it for a minute,' she said sarcastically.

'But her services are, have been and always will be confined to the secretarial, and if you had half a brain cell you'd realise that.' His face was cold now, all amusement gone. 'Anything else is purely in the fevered and definitely twisted mind of your mother.'

Melody shot a quick look over her shoulder before she hissed, 'How dare you say that? She's got more than enough to cope with at the moment without hearing her lawyer say she is a liar.'

'I'm surprised you do so well in your job if your hearing's so bad,' he said calmly. 'I didn't say she was a liar, merely that she's got a twisted mind where I'm concerned and, believe me, I could say a lot worse. She deliberately searched for a weapon to use against me from our first date and you know that as well as I do. When a piece of juicy gossip came her way, gossip completely without foundation and formed simply because Angela is a stunning-looking girl, she seized upon it with relish.'

The bit about Angela being stunning had hit her in the solar plexus like a sledgehammer. She had never wanted to hurt someone as she did Zeke right at that moment. He could stand there and defend that loathsome woman and make her sound like a saint without even blinking an eye!

'You had queues of applicants for the post of secretary when Mrs Banks retired,' she said tightly, willing her voice not to betray her hurt. 'Why did you pick Angela Brown?'

'Because she was the best,' he said in a tone which indicated he thought Melody was dim.

'You didn't tell me at the time Mrs Banks had gone and Angela had arrived,' she accused woodenly.

'Why talk business when there are a million other things vastly more interesting?'

He had an answer for everything! She just prevented herself from grinding her teeth in time. 'You took her away with you to Paris.' *Paris,* the city of lovers.

'My secretary accompanied me on a business trip abroad. That's slightly different. But we've been over all this before.' His tone took on an impatient note she remembered of old. 'I was hoping by now you would have come to your senses.'

He made it sound as if he'd searched her out! She glared at him, utterly outraged. Whereas it had been she who had contacted him about the case against her mother. From the day she had thrown his ring back at him she hadn't heard a word. Not a phone call. Not even a Christmas card. Right up until this very moment she hadn't admitted to herself just how much his complete exit from her life had hurt, but he'd cut her off as though she'd ceased to exist.

And yet… Her mind jolted. He'd been keeping tabs on her all the time. What did that indicate?

Probably that he was quite happy to frolic with Angela as long as his ex-fiancée didn't find a man to do the same with, she answered herself bitterly. And their final row hadn't only been about his affair with his secretary anyway.

As though he could read her mind, he now said, 'How's the new job shaping up anyway?'

'Hardly new. I've been there almost six months now.' She raised her chin in an unconscious gesture of defiance. 'I love it. It's fascinating.'

And it was true, she did love it. The demanding and time-consuming post specialising in working with patients whose speech was impaired by a stroke or as the result of an accident was both fascinating and rewarding, but she'd been forced to admit after a few weeks she hadn't realised just how committed she'd need to be or how the job would take over her life.

The theoretical work she had done in her degree, which had encompassed psychology, neurology and speech pathology among other things, just hadn't prepared her for how wrapped up in her patients' welfare she'd become. If someone needed extra time—time that was officially her own—she gave it gladly, and then there were the reams and reams of paperwork to wade through.

She needed to keep records which were detailed and bang up-to-date to enable her to work effectively with the team of social workers, doctors and psychologists at the hospital and health centre she was assigned to.

When the post had first been mentioned she and Zeke had just got engaged and were beginning to plan their wedding. It had caused immediate problems between them. 'I don't see you as much as I'd like to now,' he had said quietly when she'd excitedly told him about the marvelous opportunity. 'Your nature is such that you can't give anything except one hundred per cent—and I love that about you, don't get me wrong—but if you take this position I'll see you even less.'

'You don't know that,' she'd argued back, disappointed.

'The writing's on the wall, Melody. They've already admitted they're very short-staffed and that consequently the hours can be long. That was a warning, don't you see? Think about this carefully. You already do a valuable job; won't that suffice for the present, at least for a little while until we're married and settled into our new life together?'

It had sounded reasonable and she'd almost agreed then and there, but after a day or two she'd begun to feel unsettled about refusing what was a great boost to her career.

Her mother had related how she'd given up her work when she'd married Melody's father, and how much she'd regretted doing so when he had upped and left a few years later, saying she'd grown boring and dull. Zeke could do the same to Melody if she wasn't careful.

'Of course, there was another woman at the bottom of it, I know that,' her mother had said bitterly. 'It's always another woman. Men just aren't monogamous, none of them, but it keeps them on their toes if they think you're successful and independent.'

'Zeke doesn't want me to give up work,' she'd protested. 'Just not accept this new job at the moment.'

'It's the same thing.' Her mother had shaken her head. 'Don't let him think he's got you where he wants you. It's the death knell on any relationship, especially with a man like Zeke. Your father was a high-flyer too,' she'd added grimly.

It was the same thing Melody had heard to a greater or lesser extent all her life, but this time her mother's words had struck deep. Probably because she'd never met anyone she cared about as she cared for Zeke.

She looked at him now as he said, 'I'm pleased you're happy, Melody.'

Happy? She'd never be happy again but she couldn't very well tell him that. When she'd thrown him out of her life she'd thrown happiness, joy, hope, peace and a hundred other emotions besides along with him. She smiled brightly. 'Yes, I am, I'm very happy.'

He reached out a large hand and traced the shadows under her eyes. She had to force herself not to flinch from the gentle caress. 'You look tired,' he said softly.

Tired? Was that another way of saying she looked haggard? 'I've been worried about all this bother with

Julian,' she said stiffly. 'The firm's Mother's baby, as you well know. She'd be devastated if she lost it.' She didn't mention the long nights when she couldn't sleep a wink as pictures of Zeke and Angela together seared her mind.

When her mother had admitted she had paid a private investigator to check Zeke out, she hadn't been able to believe it at first. Not even when photographs of Zeke and Angela were produced. Photographs which showed them having dinner and getting into a taxi together, Angela showing an inordinate amount of leg as she did so.

She had been furious with her mother, furious with Zeke, furious with herself for being so stupid and gullible. When he'd explained about the business trip to Paris she hadn't believed it had been only business. She still didn't. The voluptuous brunette might be good at her job but the saucy tilt to her head and the way the camera had caught her looking at Zeke had spoken volumes.

Steeling her voice, she said dismissively, 'Thank you for coming here today, Zeke, and for taking the case. I mustn't keep you any longer.'

'You grow more like your mother every day.'

It wasn't meant as a compliment, it was meant to wound. And it did. Don't react. Don't give him the satisfaction of knowing you care what he thinks about you. She dredged another smile up from the depths of her. 'Thank you,' she said carefully. 'She's an amazing woman, isn't she?'

'Amazing.'

She ignored the dry note. 'Goodbye, Zeke.'

As she went to turn he surprised her by taking her arm. 'Don't you want to know the conditions attached to my taking your mother's case?' he asked smoothly.

'Conditions?' Her eyes widened in alarm. 'You never

said anything about conditions when you were talking to her in the house.'

'I didn't think you'd want me to. They're for your ears only anyway. As you've already said, she has enough on her plate at the moment and it would only worry her to know you're having dinner with me, considering she thinks I'm the Marquis de Sade and Don Juan rolled into one.'

She looked into his face, seeking visual confirmation that he was joking. He couldn't seriously be suggesting she have dinner with him, could he? Not after everything that had happened. Even Zeke Russell wouldn't be that arrogant.

'I'm quite serious, Melody.' As ever he had read her mind. 'I want to have dinner with you tonight.'

'No way.' She found her voice.

'That's a pity.' The amber eyes narrowed. 'But I can suggest an alternative lawyer for your mother.'

'You don't mean it. You wouldn't blackmail me into having dinner with you.' She studied the strong planes of his jaw, the hard cheekbones and determined chin. He meant it all right.

'Blackmail's an unacceptable word.' His smile was without humour. 'I prefer to look on it as enabling you to see reason.'

'You're crazy.' She couldn't quite believe she was having this conversation.

'Why? Because I want to put my case? I was never allowed to six months ago. Remember? Perhaps that's what's needed to clear the air so we can both move on.'

'I've already moved on.' She knew her trembling must be visible but she couldn't seem to control the shaking. This was Zeke at his most dangerous, when his voice was mild and cool and his face impassive. 'I'm doing just fine.'

'I'm glad to hear it.'

'I don't want to have dinner with you, Zeke. Can't you get that into your head? In fact you're the last man on earth I want to spend time with.' She didn't know who she was trying to convince more, him or herself.

She saw the glimmer of reaction flare in his eyes before he hid the anger, but it heartened her. How dared he think he could swan back into her life and order her about? She ignored the little fact it had been she who had summoned him.

She was unprepared for Zeke taking her into his arms and such was her surprise that for a moment she remained soft and pliant against his chest. When she began to struggle his lips took hers in the old possessive way, his mouth warm and firm. He was holding her in such a fashion she could feel what her body was doing to his but he appeared unconcerned about his arousal, his arms tightening.

His muscled strength, the clean scent of his aftershave and the warmth of his body were all painfully familiar. Familiar and intoxicating. How often had she dreamt of his kisses and caresses in the months they had been apart, only to awake with tears streaming down her face in the isolation of her bedsit?

But she couldn't respond to him. Not now, not ever. Her head was telling her one thing but her body wasn't obeying. In the past they'd only had to touch each other for fire to ignite and it looked as if that hadn't changed.

By the time Zeke raised his head her blood was singing and her head spinning, but out of some inner strength she hadn't known she possessed she had resisted the temptation to kiss him back. But he knew the effect he had on her. The knowledge was there in the satisfied tawny eyes.

Melody's head came up proudly. 'There's a name for men like you,' she said scathingly, her cheeks fiery.

'I know.' His cool glance assessed her face. 'It's called mis-judged. Now, dinner at eight, I think. I'll call round at your bedsit at seven-thirty. Be ready. I don't like to be kept waiting.'

'You can't tell me what to do.'

He smiled coldly. 'Actually I can. If you want me to help your mother, that is. Personally I think it might do Anna the world of good to lose the whole caboodle and face the fact she's human like the rest of us. She's been locked in that ivory tower she calls her business too long.'

Melody controlled her temper with extreme difficulty. She hated him. How she hated him. How could she have imagined she loved him? She was still struggling to find a suitable put-down when Zeke turned and walked to his car, calling over his shoulder, 'Seven-thirty, Melody. And dress up. We're going somewhere special.'

'You're... You loathsome...'

She was still searching for suitable adjectives when he drove away. Smiling.

CHAPTER TWO

MELODY had to stand quite still for a good thirty seconds before she could gain enough composure to turn and close the door. She walked through to the sitting room, where her mother was waiting, hiding her shaking hands by thrusting them deep into the pockets of her denim skirt.

'Has he gone?' her mother asked unnecessarily.

Melody nodded.

'It didn't go too badly, did it? He was more reasonable than I expected, all things considered.'

She nodded again.

'You were a long time seeing him off. What did you talk about?'

'Nothing much.' Melody suddenly found she couldn't discuss this any longer without screaming. 'Look, I'll talk to you later; I really do have to get to work. They were very good about giving me a few hours off but I have to be there for a couple of patient assessments this afternoon.'

'Are you all right, Melody? Zeke didn't say anything to upset you, did he?' Her mother stared at her intently.

Besides making it abundantly clear he was now in the position to call all the shots? Shots that would undoubtedly be at her expense?

'I can call this off right now if you want and let him know we won't be proceeding any further,' Anna added.

Melody grasped the opportunity to deflect her mother from insisting on an answer to her previous question. 'No you won't, Mother,' she said firmly. 'We're seeing this through to the bitter end. Julian is not going to ruin you. Whatever else Zeke is, he's a brilliant lawyer, and that's what we need.'

'Yes, I can see that.'

Her mother's immediate acquiescence revealed the extent of her worry. Melody stopped just long enough to give a little more reassurance before she left the house, but once in her car she drove automatically, her mind focusing on the evening ahead.

By the time she got to the hospital she had to admit excitement now mingled with her anger but she would have walked stark naked through the streets of London before she revealed that to a living soul. The truth was she felt more alive today than at any time in the last six months, and it was humiliating. How could she still be attracted to a man who had betrayed her? Not only betrayed her, but almost persuaded her to put her career on hold and play blissful newly-weds while he conducted a sordid liaison with his secretary. It was as her mother said—men were incapable of being monogamous. She didn't ever intend to let herself become vulnerable again with any man, and especially, *especially* Zeke Russell.

Zeke sat in his office, staring at a wad of papers on his desk, but he wasn't seeing them. Imprinted on his mind was a lovely face, the skin pale and almost translucent, the eyes dove-grey and fringed with spiky lashes, the lips a full, soft Cupid's bow. She was more beautiful than any woman had the right to be, and the irony was she didn't know it.

He had known from their first date that Melody's slim, perfect body housed a host of insecurities, some of which could be traced back to her father leaving and others which definitely could be put at her mother's feet. All through the time they'd been seeing each other, even after he'd asked her to marry him, he'd had the distinct impression she was just waiting for something to go wrong.

It had irritated him on occasion, he had to admit it, but then he hadn't realised how deep her uncertainties ran. He had thought his love would conquer everything. He smiled grimly. He had been wrong.

He stood up abruptly, walking over to the window that looked out over a busy London street, and stared down at the cars and people two floors below.

He had handled things badly, that was for sure; he'd let the accusations she'd flung at him get to him. Part of it had been anger that she didn't trust him enough to listen to what he had to say, that she'd had him hung, drawn and quartered before she even put the matter of the photographs and Angela to him. Another element had been pride. He'd been damned if he was going to crawl and plead for her to listen to him. And then there was his own disappointment and outrage. He had opened up to Melody more than anyone he'd ever known and she'd flung it all back in his face that day. He could cheerfully have throttled her at the time.

But no. He turned from the window, flinging himself down in the big leather chair and raking his hair back from his brow. He would never lay a finger on her in anger. He had nothing but contempt for men who behaved like that. But neither was he prepared to become less of a man, to beg and grovel. It felt as if he'd had his right arm cut off when she left him, but rather that than lose his self-respect. If she didn't trust him enough to at least give him the benefit of the doubt and listen to what he had to say, there was no basis for a relationship anyway.

He scowled at the inoffensive papers as a little voice in the back of his mind jibed, but you never expected her to stay away so long, did you? You thought she'd come to her senses and come back to you within the month when she'd had time to think things through. And then one month had passed, and another, and the whole thing had mushroomed. And he'd finally had to accept she had no intention of calling him or trying to put things right.

And so her mother had won. His head lifted and he stared across the room. Ironic really—he had a reputation for being the best defence lawyer around and when it had come to defending himself he'd been a non-starter. That must have given Anna Taylor some amusement.

He swore, the oath harsh and ugly, but it afforded him no relief. And now he'd agreed to defend Anna when really he would like nothing better than to see her lose everything she'd ever worked for. So why had he taken the case?

The frown deepened. Because he believed she was innocent. He loathed the woman—in fact he wouldn't have believed he could feel such intense loathing for another human being—but whatever else she was, Anna wasn't a cheat or a swindler. More was the pity. It would have been sweet to see her humbled.

As for Melody… He pressed his forefinger and thumb into the corners of his eyes and pressed hard before raising his head determinedly. He couldn't afford to give her the upper hand with his emotions again. But neither did he intend to give in and let her go. His main aim in going to her mother's house this morning had been to see her, to be close to her. That and having his curiosity satisfied. The latter had been accomplished with little effort as they'd fallen over themselves to give him all the facts; the former had told him he'd use whatever weapon he was given to continue seeing more of her. For the time being. Until he decided how this scenario was going to finally end. And this time he would be the one in control of the finale.

By the time Zeke rang the doorbell of the big old house in Finsbury where Melody had her bedsit, she knew she looked the best she could. For once her shoulder-length hair had played ball when she'd put it up in a loose knot at the back of her head, leaving her fringe and a few wispy tendrils to soften the look. Her make-up had gone on perfectly, her mascara separating and lengthening each lash instead of clogging them together as it usually did when she attempted more than one coat, and her lipstick was glossy and moist.

The dress she'd decided to wear was not a new one but she knew it suited her and she needed the confidence tonight, the charcoal velvet top and intricately beaded chiffon skirt and matching shawl glamorous but sexy and clinging in all the right places. And her perfume was perfectly delicious.

She'd been a bundle of nerves all afternoon and as jumpy as a cat on a hot tin roof, but now the moment was here, now the doorbell had rung, a fatalistic calm descended. She'd had no option about seeing him tonight so in one way that was comforting; it wasn't as though she'd had to make the decision and then worry it was the wrong one. Whatever he expected from the evening, she wasn't going to be the adoring, loving girl he'd known before their split, the girl who had been so besotted with h... been able to see straight, the girl who had worr... sick he'd get fed up with her sooner or later.

Her soft mouth drooped unknowingly.

The doorbell rang again and she walked over to the little box at the side of her front door and pressed the intercom. 'Yes?' she said quietly.

'It's Zeke.'

The deep, smoky voice set her heart thudding anew but she managed to keep her voice flat when she said, 'I'll be right down.'

Her bedsit was one of two on the top floor of the three-storey Victorian terraced house. Each floor housed two bedsits and one separate bathroom, the ground floor also boasting a large communal kitchen for all the residents' use if they so required. This was an extension to the original house and had effectively replaced the small garden.

Melody had first moved in seven years before when she had left her mother's house at the age of twenty-three. A substantial pay rise in her first job, which she'd held since leaving university, had meant she could finally afford to rent her own place.

She loved her little home. She turned now at the door to glance over the light, spacious room, the high ceiling and two large windows giving the area a capacious feel. With the landlord's permission she'd decorated as soon as she had taken up residence, painting the walls and ceiling off-white and the woodwork a pale shade of lilac that went well with the biscuit carpet.

Drifts of muslin at the windows made sure no light was lost in the day, and she'd installed off-white blinds to pull at night for privacy. The pale lilac two-seater sofa doubled as her bed and the light theme was lifted by deep lilac scatter cushions and other splashes of colour, such as the scarlet vase holding ornamental grasses at the side of the TV.

She had placed her small dining table and two chairs close to one of the windows and loved to eat gazing out over the rooftops into the wide expanse of sky. She sometimes felt as though she were sitting on top of the world. It was a peaceful home, serene, and her tiny kitchen area in one corner, holding her microwave-cum-oven, minute fridge and two-burner hob, meant she didn't have to use the kitchen at the bottom of the house at all if she didn't want to.

After closing the door she walked carefully down the narrow, steep stairs, conscious that her strappy sandals were higher than the shoes she normally wore by a good inch or two. After clicking her way across the tiled lobby she opened the front door to the house. Zeke was leaning against the railings that separated the three feet or so of paved front garden from the street, his masculine aura emphasised by the black dinner jacket and tie he was wearing.

Melody took a long, deep, hidden breath. He looked good. The understatement mocked her. And she had been existing the last six months, not living. Living was being with Zeke.

Raw panic at how she was feeling made her voice stiff when she said, 'This really isn't a good idea, you know that, don't you?' For her. In fact it was emotional suicide.

'I don't see it that way.' He levered himself upright and took her arm, his eyes stroking their amber light over her before he said, 'You look sensational.'

'Thank you.' Even to her own ears she sounded like a prim matron of advanced years, her voice clipped and short. She sucked in another breath and tried harder. 'Where are we going?'

'To the theatre first.' He mentioned a show she'd been dying to see for ages but the tickets were like gold dust. 'And then we've a table reserved at the Black Cat.'

Melody stared at him. He couldn't have produced the tickets for the theatre or the reservation at the Black Cat out of thin air at such short notice. He'd obviously been planning to take someone else tonight. Angela? A chill shivered down her spine and she felt no triumph that the other woman's nose must have been put out of joint. This was horrible, just horrible.

The tawny eyes dissected her response. Then he said softly, 'Marvin—you remember Marvin?—' Melody nodded; the man was a partner at the law firm Zeke worked for '—had planned to take his wife out on their twenty-fifth wedding anniversary tonight. Unfortunately she was rushed into hospital yesterday with gall-bladder problems. Their loss, our gain.'

'Oh, I see.' She felt like an absolute worm.

'So it wasn't a matter of disappointing one of my harem.'

He had known. She kept her expression perfectly bland. 'I don't know what you're talking about,' she lied flatly.

'Of course you don't,' he said with icy neutrality. He gestured to the waiting taxi cab. 'Shall we?'

Great start to the evening, Melody. Well done. As she climbed into the cab she was berating herself. This night was going to be difficult enough as it was without her making it worse from the outset.

As he sat down beside her in the back of the cab, she swallowed hard. 'I'm sorry,' she said in a very small voice. 'I shouldn't have jumped to the conclusion I did.'

For a moment she thought he was going to be awkward, as he had every right to be, she admitted silently. He stared at her for a second, then shook his head, expelling a long breath. 'You'll drive me mad before you're finished, woman,' he said. But his tone was rueful rather than nasty. 'Look, for the record, I'm not with anyone at the moment. OK? I haven't been with anyone since we split, in fact.'

She felt a wild thrill of joy before reason kicked in. He would say that, wouldn't he? She could almost hear her mother's voice. But it didn't necessarily make it true.

'Do you believe me?' he asked quietly, something in his tone making her look straight into his eyes.

She knew what he wanted her to say and, in view of the fact he was taking her mother's case, she ought to play ball. But she hesitated too long.

'Enough said,' he drawled dryly.

'I haven't said anything.'

'Quite.'

'Look, Zeke—' She gulped. He was very close and very big. The memory of other cab rides when she'd been locked in his embrace was hard to dispel. 'I don't want to fight with you.'

'That's nice.' The look on his face didn't fit with his words.

'What I mean is…' She floundered. What did she mean? She was darned if she knew. 'You're a free agent,' she managed at last, but weakly.

'A free agent?' He nodded. 'Yes, I'm a free agent. And I think you're trying to tell me you are too. Is that right?'

'Well…yes.' Not that it would do her any good when her heart was still irrevocably his.

'That's established that, then.' He stretched out long legs and Melody's senses went into hyperdrive.

For goodness' sake, she thought crossly, he's not even touching you and you're going to pieces.

'So, now we've affirmed we're both free agents, can you relax a little?'

He wasn't looking at her, his gaze was straight ahead, but it felt as though the laser eyes were dissecting her bit by bit. Melody wrenched her gaze from his profile. 'I'm perfectly relaxed,' she lied tensely.

'Yeah, right.'

'Anyway, how do you expect someone to feel when they're ordered out to dinner?' she snapped.

'When the dinner's at the Black Cat and the show beforehand is the one everyone's talking about?' he drawled easily. 'Grateful fits the bill.'

'*Grateful?* I don't think so.'

'Please yourself.'

He sounded supremely uninterested and it was incredibly galling. Especially because if pleasing herself came into it they would be happily married by now and living together with no thoughts of ever being apart. Don't, she warned herself fiercely. Don't go down that road. Control. This was all about control—his over hers—but she couldn't let him think he had all the trump cards.

She shrugged, forcing a nonchalant note to her voice. 'It doesn't matter anyway; it's just further proof of how very differently we see things.'

He glanced at her, a cool look that said nothing.

Goaded still further by his detachment, she added, 'We have changed. It happens all the time.'

'Like it did with your parents?'

It hit her like a blow and the shock was evident in her eyes as her gaze shot to his. 'My parents have got nothing to do with this,' she said shakily.

'No?' His eyes were unrelenting. 'I think they've got *everything* to do with it, or certainly your mother anyway. She's fed you on a diet of bitterness since you were a child but you just can't see it, can you? I don't know what went on between her and your father and I sure as hell don't want to, but one thing's for sure—she's doing her damnedest to ruin your life because of it.'

'That's not true.' Her cheeks were burning with fury. 'You haven't the faintest idea of how hard it's been for her because of him. He would have let us starve for all he cared. It was she who went out and started the business. She who provided a roof over our heads—'

'I'm not saying she didn't look after you.' He interrupted her roughly. 'I'm saying she let her own hurt and disappointment become the motive for everything she did then and still does. She doesn't like men, Melody, or haven't you noticed? They are the lowest things on planet Earth as far as your mother's concerned.'

'And can you blame her?'

'Yes, I damn well can when it impinged on me and you,' he shot back furiously.

'What happened between us—' Melody stopped abruptly as the taxi driver reached out a hand behind him and slid open the glass partition separating him from the rest of the cab.

'You might have wondered why I'm going this way, mate,' he said cheerily to Zeke. 'There's roadworks on the more direct route. Sat there for hours last night, I did.'

'*What?*' And then, as the man's words registered, Zeke moderated his voice when he said, 'Oh, that's fine; whatever way you think best.'

'Just so long as you don't think I'm pulling a fast one.'

'No, I wouldn't think that,' Zeke replied in a tone which stated he couldn't care less.

"Cos I had this right stroppy geezer in the cab last night shouting the odds. I told him, I did. I said, you get out and walk, then, mate, if you think you can get there any quicker. And do you know what the so-an'-so did?'

'Got out and walked?' Zeke said very dryly.

'Yeah, he did an' all. Without paying, the swine.'

The taxi driver's voice was so aggrieved Melody felt a well of hysterical laughter building up inside her. Here were she and Zeke discussing the breakdown of their relationship, which had afforded her such pain she hadn't thought she'd survive it in the early days, and this man was rabbiting on about a lost fare.

It was Zeke who slid the glass partition closed again and, although the taxi driver took the hint and said nothing more, silence reigned in the back of the cab until they reached the theatre. Misery sat like a rock in the pit of Melody's stomach but she pretended an interest in the view outside, the bustle of London night life ensuring there was plenty of activity.

Their theatre tickets were for the circle and turned out to be wonderful seats. Zeke bought a glossy programme and a box of chocolates for her before they sat down, and Melody buried herself in the programme in the five minutes or so before the performance began. She couldn't help but be aware of every movement Zeke made at the side of her, however, her nerves so finely tuned they were zinging. The size of him meant his thigh was touching hers, one broad shoulder wedged against her. His closeness was excruciatingly disturbing.

She had never been so glad when the lights were dimmed and the orchestra struck up—her cheeks had been burning for the whole five minutes. It hadn't helped that he'd seemed perfectly happy to sit in silence either, making no effort at conversation and apparently perfectly relaxed, if somewhat cold and grim. How she was going to get through the night she just didn't know.

However, in spite of her fevered thoughts she soon found herself taken up with the story and music on the stage about love lost and found. It was a spectacle drama with just the odd touch of comedy now and again to lighten the dark undercurrents, and she began to lose herself in the complications of the plot. When the interval arrived she couldn't believe nearly an hour had gone by.

They fought their way through throngs of people to the bar area and once Zeke had bought the drinks found a quiet corner to stand and drink them.

'Enjoying it?' Zeke asked softly, his big body shielding her from the crowd.

'Very much.' She smiled politely, a social smile.

'Good.' His mouth quirked. 'The evening's not quite so bad as you envisaged, then?'

'I didn't envisage it being bad,' she lied quickly.

'No?' It carried a wealth of disbelief.

'No. It was just I didn't like being forced into doing something, that's all.'

'You left me with no option.' The tawny gaze was watching her very closely.

Melody sipped her drink without replying. She didn't want to argue with him, she suddenly found. She just wanted to take this one night of being with him again because it would have to last the rest of her life. They were worlds apart in everything that mattered and there was no meeting point, she knew that, because fidelity was an absolute with her and always would be.

'Your hair's still like spun gold.' He lifted a tendril lying against her cheek and let it drift through his fingers.

She couldn't let him know how he affected her. 'It's too fine,' she managed weakly.

'No, it's perfect.' His eyes darkened. 'Sunlight shot through with streaks of moonbeams. I've never seen blonde hair with so many shades as yours.'

'My mother's is the same.' As soon as she'd said it she could have kicked herself. She knew her mother was a red rag to a bull as far as Zeke was concerned. In the early days she had thought the instant antagonism between the two which had occurred the first time she'd introduced them would die off as they got to know each other, but it had got worse, not better. And she had to admit her mother hadn't given Zeke a chance. He had tried, she knew that, but her mother had remained almost obsessively cool with him. He didn't know, but she and her mother had rowed about her attitude more than once.

Zeke's parents had been killed in an automobile accident three years before she met him and as he was an only child she'd wanted the three of them to hit it off, considering her mother was the only family they had between them. It wasn't until she and Zeke had split up that her mother had admitted Zeke reminded her terribly of Melody's father. 'Not just in his physique, although your father was exceptionally tall and broad,' her mother had said flatly. 'You can't see that from the photographs, not really. But the way Zeke is, his…well, charisma, drawing power, call it what you will. You know what I mean?' And then without waiting for a reply, she'd added, her tone acidic, 'And the same giant ego, of course.' They hadn't continued the conversation after that.

It had taken Melody quite a while to forgive her mother for interfering so arbitrarily in the matter of the photographs, something Anna had been well aware of. It was only the fact Melody knew her mother had thought she was doing it for the best which had enabled them to eventually get back on their old footing after three or four months.

That and her mother writing an emotional—certainly for Anna—letter stating her reasons for meddling. Anna had penned,

I didn't want you to have to go through what I did. That's why I felt I had to find out what he was really like. You might think you feel bad now, but if you had gone ahead and married him, had children, and then discovered he'd been playing around, it would have crucified you. Like it did me. I didn't want that for you. Not you.

Melody came back to the present to see Zeke's face had stiffened at the mention of her mother. Then she watched him make a visible effort to relax tense facial muscles.

His voice was deliberately without expression when he said, 'I think your hair is unique but you could be right about Anna's.' An awkward pause followed. Then he said, 'Can I get you another drink?'

She didn't really want one but she said yes anyway, hoping it would help diffuse the tension between them. Once he returned they talked of inconsequentials until the first bell rang for the second half, by which time Melody felt slightly tipsy after two glasses of wine on an empty stomach. She made a mental note to ask for fizzy water at the Black Cat before she ate her meal.

The second half of the show was even better than the first, the climax—when the young heroine gave up her sweetheart to another woman whom he had loved but thought had died years before—reducing Melody to gulping tears. She didn't refuse the large, crisp white handkerchief Zeke silently passed her as the music finished its crescendo, dabbing at her eyes and then blowing hard before she gave it back. 'That was wonderful,' she said fervently as the audience began to rise from their seats and make their way out of the theatre.

'But so sad. That poor girl, to let him go when she loved him so much.'

'It's only a story,' Zeke said softly at her side.

Maybe. As they too rose and began to wind their way to the stairs, Melody could have burst into tears again. But true to life nevertheless. She'd lost him to someone else, hadn't she?

In spite of the crowd milling about on the pavement outside the theatre, Zeke seemed to have no difficulty in hailing a cab. But then cabs, along with everything else, always seemed to be at his beck and call.

Perhaps because the performance was so fresh in her mind, once they were on their way to the nightclub Melody found herself saying, 'Life seems to be one big merry-go-round of ups and downs, don't you think?'

'To an extent. It's also what you make it.'

He spoke as if it was a criticism of what she'd said and immediately Melody's hackles rose. 'You can't always make it better or different.'

He shrugged, turning his head and looking at her properly as he slid one arm along the back of the seat. She sat perfectly still, vitally aware of the feel and smell of him.

'Occasionally that might be true,' he said conversationally, his easy nonchalance at odds with her tight voice. 'In the case of a serious illness, for example, or the death of a loved one. Even then how you tackle such things has a bearing on the way you feel whatever the outcome. Bitterness, rage, resentment are all killers. If they take root they colour everything.'

Melody stared at him. He was definitely having a dig at her here, she just knew it, or was she being paranoid? Either way she couldn't rise to it because he'd just say if the cap fits, wear it. She wriggled slightly. He was the most irritating man in the world.

'You don't agree?' he asked silkily.

'So you're saying whatever anyone does to another person, however bad a situation they find themselves in or whatever goes wrong in their life, they're supposed to grin and bear it?' she prevaricated. 'Water off a duck's back and all that?'

'Of course not.' His voice had now taken on a note which suggested he was dealing with a recalcitrant child.

The taxi chose that particular moment to draw up outside the Black Cat, one of London's most prominent nightclubs. Melody wasn't sorry. The conversation had been most unsettling, but then that was Zeke all over. She'd also felt she was definitely on a loser and that wasn't good.

She wasn't aware she was frowning as Zeke helped her out of the cab until he murmured, 'Could you at least try and look as though you're pleased to be here? The management isn't used to people looking daggers as they enter the place, not at the price they charge, anyway, and when there's a waiting list an arm long for a table.'

She said something very rude about the management that shocked them both, and her cheeks were bright pink as she entered the building on Zeke's arm.

Once inside she found the place to be all chrome and silver, mirrors everywhere and a general air of chic stylishness pervading the air. Their table was in a very nice spot close to the small dance floor but set back slightly in one of the alcoves dotted about the room. It gave a degree of privacy whilst still being at the hub of everything.

Melody sank into her seat and couldn't help sniffing the air slightly as a bevy of delicious aromas came her way. She was ravenous and, from what she'd seen of the food on the way to their table, everything looked wonderful. She was blessed with a metabolism which enabled her to eat like a horse and still not put on weight, but the other side of the coin was she could feel giddy and sick if the time was too long between meals. Like now.

The wine waiter appeared at their sides and Zeke ordered a bottle of the expensive claret which had been their favourite when they were seeing each other, as well as a bottle of the sparkling water she'd requested. As a basket of warm rolls were placed on the table, Zeke said quietly, 'Eat one now; your blood sugars are low, aren't they?'

Melody nodded. She'd forgotten how nice it was to be looked after. He'd always noticed if she was feeling unwell or something was wrong without having to be told; none of the men she'd dated before Zeke had been so intuitive. But then she hadn't let any of them into her life as she had Zeke and certainly none of them had stirred her blood as he had.

Before she had met him she'd always considered herself something of a cold fish in the sex department. She definitely hadn't jumped in and out of bed with each boyfriend, as several of her friends seemed to think was perfectly normal. She simply hadn't been tempted to.

It had been different with Zeke. For the first time the dream she'd had since being a little girl of walking down the aisle in a fluffy white dress knowing her wedding night would be special was challenged by her own need and desire.

When they had first begun dating she had shyly told him she wanted to keep herself for marriage and a husband. He hadn't laughed or derided her, as one or two previous boyfriends had done. Neither had he tried to persuade her to change her mind. It had been she who had wavered, on more than one occasion, when his lovemaking had been so wonderful she had wanted it all. The only thing he'd ever said—on the evening he'd presented her with a magnificent diamond ring and asked her to marry him—was that it would need to be a short engagement. A man could only take so many cold showers a night.

She'd laughed then, hugging him and agreeing they would set the date for two months ahead, which would just give them time to find a church and for her to buy her dream dress. She hadn't wanted a huge wedding with all the frills; just Zeke, being married in a special setting and wearing the dress of her imagination.

And then she'd found out about Angela.

She spread the roll liberally with butter and took a bite of the fragrant, warm bread. It was delicious but her thoughts had dulled her taste buds.

'So the job's good?' he asked suddenly, surprising her into looking at him.

Her mouth full of bread, she nodded.

'Hectic?'

She swallowed. 'Very.' She decided honesty was the best policy. 'Twelve hours a day when it's necessary,' she said quietly, 'but that's not all the time.' Most of it, but not all. 'I couldn't have done it if we'd still...' She stopped, aware she was being tactless.

'Been together?' he finished for her.

She nodded again. 'The people who work on the unit are single or have very understanding partners,' she admitted.

The wine waiter appeared with their bottle and, after he had poured them both a glass and vanished again, Zeke drank half a glass straight down before he said, his fingers toying with his bread plate, 'I was too hasty about that, on reflection.'

Melody stared at him before she realised her mouth had fallen open in a slight gape and couldn't look very nice, full as it was with the last of the roll. She shut it with a little snap, swallowed the bread and said, 'Actually you were probably right. The first three months were exhausting and all I did was work and sleep. It wouldn't have been the best start to a marriage.'

'Don't argue,' he said with a smile which faded as he continued, 'I realised afterwards it was a great opportunity for you and one which might not have occurred again for a long time. You were right to take it. The least I could have done would be to have had a hot meal waiting for you when you walked in, followed by a long soak in the tub and maybe a massage on any tense muscles.'

He was half joking but it sounded so heavenly she couldn't summon up the required smile. Instead she felt her eyes fill with tears and, horrified, quickly looked down at her plate. 'It's water under the bridge now,' she managed fairly steadily. 'Unimportant.'

'I guess so. I just wanted you to know, that's all.'

Something in his voice made her want to raise her eyes and take his hand but the image of Angela Brown stopped her. The pert, beautiful face of the sexy brunette was there on the screen of her mind and for the life of her she couldn't move a muscle.

The arrival of their first course, a platter of seafood garnished with lemon wedges and lamb's lettuce and accompanied by wholemeal bread, all of which went under the exotic name of *fruits de mer*, couldn't have arrived at a better moment. By the time the bustling waiter had arranged the accompaniments to his satisfaction Melody had gained control of herself. She had imagined the vulnerability in his voice, she told herself firmly as she speared a succulent prawn with her fork. Of course she had.

Rib of beef with mustard crust and saffron mash followed the seafood, and Melody allowed herself a glass of the claret with this. It all tasted divine. She said as much to Zeke and he grinned. 'I ought to be feeling sorry for poor old Marvin and his wife but I'm too selfish,' he admitted unrepentantly. 'It's not often a gift from the gods falls into one's lap at such a perfect time.'

'Perfect time?'

'When I'd managed to get you to go out to dinner with me.'

He made it sound as though he'd been asking her for months, Melody thought with a dart of resentment. And because the wine had loosened her tongue, she said, 'Perhaps I would have gone out to dinner with you before if you had asked.' She said it lightly, almost flirtatiously, but the small throb at the back of her voice caught Zeke's attention.

The golden gaze fastened on her face and studied it for a moment. 'You left me, remember?' he said very softly. 'I wasn't the one who said I'd made the biggest mistake of my life. I loved you. I didn't change.'

The sheer audacity had her speechless for a moment and then her eyes glowed dangerously. *'You were seeing another woman,'* she ground out furiously, and then, when he made a gesture of denial, she hissed, 'and anyway, if you loved me so much, why didn't you try and see me? Why didn't you come after me?'

'So you could scream insults at me again?' She could see fire at the back of his gaze now but he controlled his anger better than she did and his voice was perfectly calm. 'No way. I had done nothing wrong and I was damned if I was going to beg. From the first moment I laid eyes on you there was no one else and I thought you'd work that out for yourself, given time.'

The way he said it, the ring of truth in his voice made

Melody blink. Sometimes during the long, lonely nights she had asked herself if she could possibly have got it wrong. OK, so he hadn't told her his old secretary had been replaced by Miss Hot-Lips, but maybe, as he'd said, he'd considered it unimportant? And maybe Angela *had* been the best applicant for the job? And maybe the Paris trip *had* been purely business? And maybe those sizzling photographs where the other woman had fairly smouldered *had* been completely innocent? But she'd always been forced to reach the same conclusion. There were just too many maybes.

'And if we're talking whys,' he continued in the same reasonable, quiet voice, 'why didn't you at least see Angela and ask *her* if we were having an affair?'

Was he stark, staring mad? Why on earth would she give the woman that satisfaction? 'Like you would another man if the boot was on the other foot and you thought I'd had an affair?' she bit out sarcastically.

'Oh, I'd see the guy, make no mistake about that, Melody,' he said even more softly. 'And if I found out it was true he'd wish he'd never been born.'

She blinked again. The wave of energy as he'd spoken was so fierce it was palpable. She took a gulp of wine. 'Yes, well, men and women deal with these things differently.'

'Wrong.' He eyed her with definite hostility. 'Ninety-nine per cent of the population would deal with it one way, *my* way. You, on the other hand, are the one per cent that's off the wall. You fling accusations around which can't be substantiated because I know for a fact they're damn well not true, you break off our engagement and then take yourself out of my life for good and you don't ask for any proof one way or the other.'

'I had the photographs—'

'Don't make me laugh. If every man and woman who share a taxi were accused of having an affair there'd hardly be anyone left. We had a long business meeting and then our hosts gave us dinner before calling a taxi to take us back to the hotel. End of story. And if I remember rightly I was champing at the bit to get back to you so bad, I caught the first flight home at the crack of dawn the next morning and left Angela to tie up the loose ends and fly back later in the day. Hardly the actions of a besotted lover making the most of a bit on the side,' he finished baldly. 'And all this could have been confirmed at the time if you'd bothered to ask. But you didn't care that much, did you? That's it in a nutshell.'

'That's so unfair.' She felt numb. His words had cut so deeply they'd eradicated all feeling.

'Melody, I gave you all of me but you kept back a large part of yourself from day one,' he said relentlessly. 'Just in case.'

'In case? I don't know what you're talking about.'

'Then let me enlighten you. In case I behaved as all men are programmed to behave from birth—according to your mother, that is—and messed around.'

Under the table her hands were clenched into fists so tightly the nails were biting into her palms. She wanted to deny it, she wanted to tell him he was crazy, but she couldn't. For the first time she acknowledged he was right; she *had* behaved as he'd described. She hadn't been aware of it but that was the motive which had prevented her from having a full relationship in the physical sense with anyone before Zeke, and especially, *especially* with him. And emotionally she'd always been ultra-wary too. Even suspicious.

She reached out a hand and lifted her wine glass, draining it before she put it down.

For right or wrong she knew she couldn't give her body to a man without giving him heart, soul and mind too. This hadn't mattered before Zeke—it had been easy to keep herself aloof then—but with him… And in spite of the agonising pain when she had seen the photographs, she recognised now there had been an element of relief too. The worst had happened. She didn't have to live each day fearing he would tire of her once they were married. Fearing she would be left with little ones as her mother had been, or, worse, that she would love him so much she would stay with him whatever and lose every bit of herself that made her her.

She wiped her mouth with her napkin. She was a mess, a head case.

'More wine?' His voice was cool and, as she raised her eyes to the amber gaze, it struck her afresh how devastatingly attractive he was.

Speaking was beyond her right at that moment and so she merely nodded. She watched him as he filled her glass and then sat looking broodingly across the room, his eyes slightly narrowed and his jaw uncompromising. Why it should be that moment that told her he was innocent of all charges she didn't know, but suddenly she believed him. Perhaps she'd always believed him somewhere in the depths of her, she thought wildly.

He was all she had ever imagined in a man and yet she had let him slip from her grasp. Not even slip—she had thrown him away. And how could she begin to explain that the intensity of the love she'd felt for him had scared her to death? She'd always associated love with pain and loss, with one person taking and the other giving. This concept had been birthed in her even before her father had left and her mother had become eaten up with bitterness against the male sex. Even though she'd been a small child when he'd walked out on them for another woman, she could dimly recall echoes of the terrible rows they'd had before that time. And her mother's endless weeping. There was something else too, something that had happened then that was important, but it was on the edge of her consciousness and she couldn't bring the memory to the surface.

'Are you all right?' Melody was unaware of the expression on her face but as Zeke turned his gaze back to her he was shocked for a second at the raw emotion mirrored there. 'Look, forget what I said.' His voice was rough but not unkind. 'I brought you here tonight so we could enjoy an evening together for old times' sake, not for post-mortems.' This wasn't quite true but he wasn't about to admit it.

She seemed to make a visible effort to focus on him and her voice was husky when she said, 'I *am* sorry if I hurt you, Zeke. And I *did* care.'

He wanted to say 'But not enough and certainly not like I cared for you', but he didn't. Partly because the waiter was approaching with the dessert menu and partly because he was sick of going over the same ground. She was always going to think of him as a low-life; perhaps it was better to cut his losses and walk away and be done with it. Damn it, there were other women out there. He knew several who would be happy to fill her shoes if he called them. Women who would be up for a good time with no strings attached, who enjoyed a romp in bed and male company, but didn't want the complications of heavy commitment interfering with their lives and careers. Maybe he should start a relationship with one of them.

But he wouldn't.

He took the menu from the waiter with a nod of thanks and opened it.

CHAPTER THREE

MELODY awoke very early the next morning and, despite it being the first Saturday in weeks that some urgent case or other didn't necessitate her going into work, she couldn't go back to sleep. Immediately her eyes had opened she'd thought of Zeke—even before that because she was sure she'd dreamt of him all night but she couldn't remember the details—and after tossing and turning for half an hour she admitted defeat and slid out of bed.

After rolling up the blinds she stared out into a perfect May morning, the sky cornflower-blue with the prerequisite cotton-wool cloud in residence and sunlight just beginning to spill onto the window sills. She opened the windows wide to catch the fresh air and then turned the bed back into a sofa and made some coffee, carrying a mug to the dining table and sitting down with a deep sigh.

She'd made such a hash of things. She sipped at the scalding-hot liquid, her eyes following a lone pigeon on a roof some distance away that was tucking into some morsel or other it had brought up from the street below. And it was too late, months too late to set things right. Even if she dared to try, which she didn't. Zeke would never forgive her for believing the worst about him with such alacrity and she couldn't blame him. And even if by some miracle he did forgive her, she'd managed to sour their relationship to the point of non-recovery.

Did she still believe she had been wrong and he had been telling the truth in the cold light of day? She made herself examine the facts, ruthlessly picturing the photographs—which had long since been destroyed but which were engraved on the screen of her mind—in all their glory. They still had the power to hurt her but in a different way now because they were testimony to her foolishness. She believed him. Endless ages too late, but she believed him.

By the third mug of coffee the sun was well and truly up and sailing in an azure sky, and Melody had had a good cry and dried her eyes before repeating the process. She had never felt so wretched in all her life. She would have sworn on oath she couldn't have felt worse than when she made the decision to leave Zeke, but she had been wrong. What she felt now was worse, ten times worse.

She ran a tired hand over her face, draining the last of the coffee and then standing to her feet. 'Enough,' she said out loud. 'You'll drown yourself in self-pity and guilt. Now take a shower and wash your hair and then go out and do some shopping.' A busy week had meant her provisions were non-existent, the tiny fridge holding half a pint of milk and nothing else. She didn't even have a slice of bread for some toast before she left.

Once under the shower she indulged in an extra-long soak, knowing Caroline—the young marketing executive who occupied the other bedsit on that floor—wouldn't poke her nose out of bed till midday. Later if she had her current boyfriend staying over.

After padding back to her room she dried her hair and

then had a bowl of muesli with the last of the milk. It looked and tasted like the sweepings from a rodent's cage but the penance suited her mood that morning.

She was such a coward on top of everything else, she thought as she washed up the bowl and mug. She should have said something to Zeke last night, at least let him know that she had been wrong, but although she'd come close umpteen times she just hadn't been able to force the words out. She'd told herself it wasn't the right time when they'd been dancing, and again in the taxi home, but then even when he had seen her to her door she'd fluffed it. Maybe if he had kissed her or at least appeared as if he wanted to she might have attempted it, but since their earlier conversation over dinner he'd maintained an easy, pleasant but definitely slightly detached attitude.

He didn't want her any more. He didn't really care about her personally. Asking her out, or rather *demanding* that she go out with him last night, she corrected, had been merely because he wanted to have his say about what had happened between them. He'd made his point, thrown in that she was a nutcase for good measure and then that had been that. She shouldn't be surprised. Six months with him had been enough to inform her that when a person blotted their copybook with Zeke they didn't get a second chance.

The telephone rang and she groaned out loud. Another emergency at work, she could guarantee it. Normally she wouldn't mind but today it was too much. She took a deep breath and let it out evenly. She was a professional, she told herself firmly, and much more than that to some of her patients. Friend, counsellor, confidant, encourager; some of the folk she dealt with were coping with the most frightening and demoralising experience of their lives and they needed to know someone was well and truly in their corner. And regardless of how she felt she owed them that support.

She picked up the phone, her voice in work mode as she said crisply, 'Melody Taylor. Can I help you?'

'I think so.'

A knife twisted in her heart. 'Zeke?' she said carefully. 'Is anything the matter?'

'You could say that.'

He wasn't going to take the case after all. This was her punishment. Melody tried to formulate some words but the lump in her throat blocked them. After swallowing it down she managed to croak, 'What is it?'

'*It* is the weekend, Saturday to be precise. And once the day draws to a close and evening takes over the city will party. And that's fine, just as it should be, except for the little problem that I find myself minus a partner of the opposite sex to party with.' There followed the merest pause. 'That's where you come in,' he added smoothly.

'Me?' It was a squeak.

'Just so.'

He sounded confident and self-assured and it grated on her taut nerves like barbed wire. She held the phone away from her ear for a second and glared at it. Here was she, eating her heart out, and he didn't seem to have a care in the world!

It was unfair and irrational, she knew that, but somehow his equanimity jarred. It certainly hadn't taken him long to get over her. 'But we're not seeing each other any more,' she said, stating the obvious.

'Exactly.'

She wrinkled her brow.

'If I ask anyone else out they'll have certain expectations, at the very least that I'm interested in them, and I haven't got time for that right now. Work commitments,' he added by way of explanation.

'Oh.' So what was she? A lump of wood?

'You, on the other hand, made it very clear when we split that you'd rather walk through coals of fire than countenance continuing our relationship. That having been said, I think we enjoyed each other's company when we were dating, didn't we? It would be a shame not to be friends now.'

Friends? Was he mad? She could never be Zeke's friend—well, not *just* his friend anyway.

'So, you see, it's perfect. We both know where we stand and yet we can still have fun, on a purely platonic level, of course. Until the situation alters.'

'Alters?' she asked weakly.

'One of us might meet someone,' he said so cheerfully she could have strangled him. 'And of course this person might not understand our situation.'

She didn't doubt it because she certainly didn't understand it. Her teeth clenched hard in her jaw. 'I'm not sure this is a good idea,' she ground out stonily. 'Not for us.'

'Because you don't trust me and think I'm the lowest of the low?'

His voice held an inflexion she couldn't quite put her finger on.

'But it doesn't matter now, don't you see? I don't approve of lots my friends get up to but that's their business. When something's not a heart thing it takes the sting out of it.'

Melody had just mustered the courage to chip in and tell him she *did* trust him and it was she who had made the mistake but his latter words hit that on the head. Not a heart thing. Well, that told her, didn't it?

'Not that I did anything you wouldn't have approved of,

of course, but that's old history and we agreed last night we wouldn't go there any more.'

Had they? She couldn't remember that.

'So, I can expect you'll be ready about nine tonight for the party at Brad's, then?'

Brad. His best friend. Who would no doubt be furious with her for how she'd treated Zeke. 'Tonight's not good for me,' she said levelly.

'You owe me, Melody.' His voice had changed. 'I'm doing your mother a favour in taking her case. I'm stacked up to the eyeballs as it is.'

'So friends blackmail other friends into doing what they want, do they? Charming.' Her tone was acidic. 'Your idea of friendship is not mine.'

'I don't doubt that for a minute,' he returned silkily. Another pause followed, longer this time. 'Do I pick you up?' he asked when her nerve cells were screaming.

She conceded defeat. She wanted to see him, she couldn't believe how much she wanted to see him, but not in the cold-blooded way he'd outlined. If he had called to say he'd been thinking about her all night and couldn't they talk about things she would have been in seventh heaven, she admitted miserably. As it was… 'I'll be ready for nine,' she mumbled flatly.

'Very graciously said.'

Sarcastic swine. For a minute she wished she was back to thinking the worst of him because it had made it easier to tell herself she hated him then. Not that she'd ever believed it, of course, but she'd kept trying. 'Won't Brad think it a bit odd when we turn up together?' she asked frostily.

'Possibly.'

'So are you going to call him and explain how things are?' she persisted. 'It will save explanations later. You can leave out the bit about the blackmail if you want,' she added pointedly.

'You really do like that word, don't you?' He sounded amused.

'I don't like what it means.' Her level tone was more chilling than blatant rage.

'And I don't like being labelled a heartless Lothario, so we all have our crosses to bear. Nine o'clock, Melody, and be ready.' The phone went dead.

She spent the next ten minutes prowling about the bedsit muttering curses before flinging on a pair of jeans and a little top and going out for the shopping.

The city air was warm with the tang of traffic fumes at its base, and the world and his wife were out. The small supermarket two streets away from where she lived was packed with people, and after purchasing what she needed there she stopped at the stall on the corner and bought her fruit and vegetables. By the time she was strolling home she felt calmer.

She had to look at this positively, she told herself as she entered the downstairs lobby. OK, so Zeke was calling all the shots but he *had* agreed to help her mother. Which was the main thing.

Once in the bedsit she stowed the shopping away and made more coffee, her thoughts churning on. He was obviously well and truly over her although she knew her lack of trust had got under his skin; his actions now told her that if nothing else. He was taking great delight in making her squirm.

She would have to admit she had been wrong and that she'd misjudged him. It wouldn't change much but at least her apology might appease him a little. Anyway, she owed him a bit of grovelling, all things considered, although she still thought it had been the height of stupidity not to mention he'd changed secretaries.

Oh, Zeke, Zeke. Suddenly the loss of him welled up to unbearable intensity. If only she could turn back the clock. She should have known he wouldn't engage in anything so sordid as the equivalent of a dirty weekend. She should have flung the photographs back at her mother and told her to ask Zeke about them if she was concerned, because she, Melody, was most certainly not. The wonder of hindsight!

The ring of the phone made her groan out loud. It *had* to be work calling this time. She just hoped they didn't want her involved in something which would stretch into the evening because Zeke would never believe her, she thought as she picked up the telephone. She heard her mother's voice with a feeling of relief which was tempered by her previous musings.

'Melody? Is that you?'

Who else would be answering the phone in her bedsit at ten o'clock in the morning? 'Yes, Mother,' she said quietly, trying not to let the irritation show.

'I just popped the rest of the papers Zeke wanted round to his office and he said he'd just got off the phone to you. He also said you had dinner with him last night. Are you out of your mind?'

She didn't have to take this. Melody's soft, full mouth tightened. 'No, I'm quite sane,' she said crisply.

'Then why on earth did you agree to see him last night? That's the height of foolishness. Surely you can see that? You're not going to be so stupid as to let him inveigle his way back into your life, are you? Not after the way he's behaved. The man's a womaniser—it's written all over him. He's not to be trusted.'

'I think it a little strange that you can say that when

you've effectively entrusted your good name and your business to him.' Her heart was racing and she found she couldn't breathe normally. She didn't want to argue with her mother.

'That's quite different and you know it.'

There was silence for a few moments and Melody made no effort to break it.

'I admit Zeke is good at what he does,' her mother said stiffly after a full thirty seconds had ticked by. 'I've never denied that.'

'Was he satisfied with the papers you gave him this morning?' Melody asked evenly, hoping to deflect the conversation into safer channels.

'I think so.' And then her mother's voice came soft and intense when she said, 'Don't make another mistake, Melody. Not with a man like him. What he's done once, he'll do again.'

'Like…like Dad?' Her heart was thudding like a sledgehammer now. They never spoke of him. She had grown up knowing she mustn't say his name although she couldn't remember her mother specifically instructing so. It had just been one of those unwritten and unspoken rules which instinct taught so well. She knew her father had gone off with another woman and divorced her mother as soon as he could, and also that he had never made any effort to see his only daughter. Beyond that, nothing.

As Melody waited for her mother to answer a strange feeling came over her. For a moment she almost felt as if she was suffocating. A sense of foreboding was so strong she could taste it.

'Yes.' When the reply came it was clipped and sharp.

'Zeke's not like him.'

'Zeke is *just* like him.' Her mother's voice was icy.

'Open your eyes, girl. Don't bury your head in the sand. I did that once and lived to regret it. Oh, your father could tell a good story and make you believe black was white. He had all the charm in the world. Even when I had undeniable proof he was a serial adulterer I couldn't bring myself to believe it. I didn't *want* to believe it. And then his latest trollop came to the house, ranting and raving—'

'I'm sorry.' The agony in her mother's voice was too painful to listen to. 'I didn't mean to upset you.'

'She was three months pregnant and he'd promised to marry her.' Her mother continued as if she hadn't heard Melody. 'He'd told her we were in the middle of a divorce. We soon were, of course. I heard later the girl lost the baby and not too long after that your father went abroad. He was a devil of a man, Melody. A devil. I've heard women speak of men who've knocked them about or who are unreasonable or possessive but your father was none of those things. He was much, much worse. He made you love him. He made you think you were everything to him, the luckiest woman in the world when all the time... He had no heart, no conscience.'

'You loved him very much.'

'Blindly, with all my heart. I thought I couldn't live without him. Whenever we rowed he'd talk me round because subconsciously I *wanted* to believe him. If, as he often did, he left the house for a few hours after an argument I thought the end of the world had come.'

She could remember those times, dimly, as if through a veil. And there was something else, something she couldn't quite recall. Melody screwed up her eyes. What was it? She knew it was important but it was buried so deep all she had was a terrible sensation of panic.

'Please don't see Zeke any more, Melody, even if it is as friends, as he said this morning. Men like him don't have women friends. Women are for one purpose only.'

Her mother's voice was soft and pleading now and not like her at all. There was no doubting her sincerity. And Melody knew it was only concern for her that prompted her mother to speak as she did. Nevertheless she couldn't concur and agree not to meet Zeke again, much as she didn't want to hurt her mother. And it wasn't only so that they'd retain him as her mother's lawyer either. She *wanted* to see him, needed to. She had to find out if there was any way at all they could remain in each other's worlds. Not as lovers—she knew she had blown the romantic element—but maybe as friends, as he'd proposed. He'd only suggested it to exact his last ounce of flesh for how she had behaved, she knew that, but perhaps if she hung in there some spark of regard might grow?

'Melody? Will you promise me not to see him on a social level?'

'I can't do that.' She found it terribly hard to refuse her mother and the strange feeling was back stronger than ever, causing her to almost choke as her heart pounded so hard it cut off her air supply. 'I'm sorry but I can't. But you needn't worry. He's already made it quite plain he doesn't think of me in that sense any more. What we had is gone, believe me.'

'Do you really mean that?'

'Yes, I do.' She spoke with grim finality.

'It's the best thing, dear.' Her mother didn't pretend to hide her relief. 'After those photographs and all.'

It was on the tip of Melody's tongue to say she believed the photographs had been taken completely out of context but she restrained herself just in time. It was enough for now for her mother to come to terms with the fact that Zeke was back in her life. She'd tell her she no longer believed he was guilty at some other point.

'Look, I have to go, Mother. I promised a few of the girls we'd meet up for lunch if I wasn't working.' This had the advantage of being true. 'I'll ring you tomorrow.'

Their goodbyes said, Melody put the phone down and sat staring into space for a good five minutes. The last six months without Zeke had been horrendous but at least they had held a certain tranquillity. Now the world was upside down again and she felt she was in the eye of a hurricane. One false move and she'd be swept up into the vortex, and who knew whether she'd survive the drop when it eventually spat her out?

And on that comforting note she got up to get ready for her lunch date with her friends.

CHAPTER FOUR

ZEKE arrived early, and half an hour was a long time when through sheer exhaustion you'd fallen asleep in the chair and only awoken fifteen minutes before.

Melody heard his voice on the other end of the door intercom with a feeling of doom. She was standing in her bathrobe and was still damp from the quick shower she'd indulged in, her hair tousled and not a scrap of make-up on her face. Fortunately she knew what dress she was wearing.

She glanced at the cream wool-mix dress with plunging neckline that she planned to team with a wide tan leather belt and vertiginous strappy tan sandals. The dress was hanging on the outside of the built-in wardrobe in one corner of the room and didn't look anything until it was on. Then it clung in all the right places with a slight flare in the skirt that emphasised the tiny waist the belt gave her. It was also one Zeke hadn't seen her in before and she wanted maximum impact tonight. At least that had been the plan. Now he was going to see her looking as though she was something the cat had dragged in.

'Melody?' His voice expressed patience. 'Can I come up?'

'What? Oh, yes, yes, come up,' she said, flustered. 'I'm not ready yet, though. I…I fell asleep.'

'Obviously eaten up with excitement at the thought of an evening out with your ex.'

It was said lazily but she could tell he was annoyed. For some reason it was intensely heartening. She didn't bother to analyse why in the rush to at least comb her hair before he put in an appearance.

She'd opened the bedsit door for him so when a knock sounded a few moments later he was already standing in the doorway. 'Hello,' he said softly. Then he grinned, one dark brow rising. 'When you said you weren't ready you meant it, didn't you?'

She flushed. The amber gaze seemed to penetrate the folds of her bathrobe and suddenly her nakedness beneath it was a problem. 'I fell asleep,' she said again, inanely, before recovering her wits enough to add, 'Sit down and I'll get you a coffee.' She'd have to take her things and get ready in the bathroom; there was nothing else for it because she certainly wasn't parading around in front of him in the altogether, she decided as she made the coffee.

She had the idea Zeke knew exactly how she was feeling and was loving every minute. Funny how he was being so uncompromising and hard to handle with her when he'd been so sweet in the past. He must bear her a great deal of animosity for how she'd treated him, she thought grimly. But then she'd probably be the same if it was the other way round.

Before she lost her nerve again she took the plunge as she handed him a steaming mug. 'Zeke, I just want you to know I made a mistake about the photographs and everything. I don't believe you were having an affair with Angela.'

He didn't say anything, taking the coffee but otherwise sitting quite still and surveying her with cool amber eyes.

'I just wanted you to know that,' she said uncomfortably after a few moments had ticked by.

'You don't have to lie, Melody.' His voice was expressionless, showing no emotion at all. 'I've told you I'll deal with your mother's case.'

'I'm not saying it for that.' She was stung that he thought so.

'Then why?' he asked quietly, unmoved by her indignation.

'Because I mean it.'

'I don't think so.' He took a sip of the coffee but the tawny gaze didn't leave her face. 'You broke off our engagement on the strength of what you believed, so why the sudden turn-around now? Nothing's changed.'

How could she explain to him what she didn't understand herself? She didn't know why the realisation that she'd been wrong had come like a bolt of lightning, but it had. Perhaps it was the months they'd been apart or maybe the fact that deep, deep down she'd never fully accepted he could do something like that. She didn't know. 'I've...I've had time to think,' she managed weakly.

'And if your mother hadn't been in a pickle with the business you would have contacted me, would you?' He snorted. 'I think not. Yesterday at the house and again in the evening you were still spitting bricks.'

'Yes, I know, because I hadn't...' Her voice dwindled away. She could talk until she was blue in the face and he wouldn't believe a word of it; his eyes told her so. 'Look, I don't like all this—'

'Now, that's nearer the truth.' He cut in on what she'd been about to say in true lawyer style.. 'You don't want to be in the position you find yourself in with me.' Thick black lashes swept down, hiding his gaze from her.

'Tough,' he added grimly. 'Everything in life has to be paid for.'

'We will pay you; I thought we'd made that clear.' She'd been about to say she didn't like all the bad feeling between them and that she knew it was all her fault, that she'd give the world to undo all the hurt she'd caused, but she was darned if she would now. He didn't want to listen to her, he'd made that clear, and she wasn't going to crawl. Not even for Zeke. 'I don't know why you're being like this,' she said flatly.

'Like what?' The golden gaze swept her flushed face again. 'I've taken your mother's case, I've asked you out to dinner and now to a party—and as a friend, don't forget that. I'm not insisting we finish the night in bed. I don't consider all that so very terrible. Admittedly I've used a little…leverage, but you wouldn't have come otherwise. At the moment it suits me to have a beautiful companion on my arm with whom there is no possibility of a romantic entanglement. However you see things, you owe me that.'

She couldn't believe this was Zeke talking. Zeke, who had always been so passionate, so warm, so amorous and sensual. At times his lovemaking had taken her to the brink of fulfilment and it had only been her wish to keep herself for their wedding night which had prevented consummation of their love. And now all that had been turned off by that razor-sharp, analytical brain. Had it really been love before or had he mistaken lust for love? Perhaps he'd discovered that when they'd parted? Perhaps she'd done him a favour in the long run?

She blinked back the bitter tears until she could escape to the refuge of the bathroom, gathering up her things without saying anything more beyond a quick, 'I'll be back in a few minutes,' before she left the room.

Once in the bathroom, however, she refused to give way to weeping. She'd done enough crying over the last months to fill the ocean and enough was enough. Zeke was waiting and she was blowed if she was going to walk back in there with pink-rimmed eyes. She called on the harsh training of her childhood when she'd learnt from an early age to put a brave face on things and show no emotion because her mother didn't like it if she did. That was another thing she'd come to understand through intuition alone.

She slipped into her dress, fastening the belt and then pulling on the sandals before brushing her hair into a sleek bob that just skimmed her shoulders. She didn't usually wear much make-up; her skin only needed the lightest touch of foundation and her fair lashes a coating of mascara. Tonight, though, like the night before, she made a little more effort, adding eyeshadow and a second coat of mascara along with a new plum lipstick she'd bought the week before.

Her toilet completed, she stared at herself in the mirror for a moment. She appeared to be cool and contained as she always did, and not for the first time she reflected it was amazing how her churning emotions never showed on the outside. But it had been Zeke who had really begun her emotional awakening right from their first date; she had been crazy about him from the word go, even though the intensity of her feelings had scared her to death.

In fact when she thought about it she hadn't known a moment's peace from the first day she'd met him. She had imagined love to be a wonderful, wildly exciting, exhilarating and magical experience, and it had been all those things. She just hadn't reckoned on the other side of the coin, which had been gnawing anxiety and unspoken dread that one day he would leave her for someone else.

A tap on the bathroom door and Caroline's voice calling, 'Melody? I presume that's you in there? Are you going to be long?' brought her out of her wool-gathering and back into the real world.

She opened the door by way of reply, smiling at the tall redhead as she said, 'Just leaving.'

'Wow! You look great.' Caroline's big blue eyes had opened wide, her tone gleeful as she continued, 'Don't tell me! You've got a date. At last. I told you you had to get back into the swing of things now Mr Zipper's history, didn't I?'

Mr Zipper was Caroline's caustic nickname for Zeke, so coined after their split because—as the redhead had declared when Melody had asked her about the name—the man was incapable of keeping a certain part of his anatomy in his trousers.

'You told me all right,' Melody murmured feelingly. 'About ten times a week, as I recall.'

'I'm glad to see you've taken my advice.' Caroline grinned at her. 'There's so many fish in the sea it's just not true and I hated to see you stranded in the shallows when you should be swimming in the deep blue yonder. Talking of swimming—' she lowered her voice, her eyes sparkling '—you ought to see the hunk occupying half of *my* bed at the moment. He's George Clooney meets Orlando Bloom with just a smidgen of Brad Pitt thrown in for good measure. And insatiable.' She rolled wicked eyes. 'We've been in bed since ten last night and I haven't slept a wink. I'm positively exhausted.'

Melody laughed; she couldn't help it. The other girl loved to shock and always spoke in the most outrageous terms, her giddy manner, spiky red hair and tendency towards the gothic hiding a very astute mind and above-average intelligence. Caroline held down a good job in television and yet her considerable salary seemed to slip through her fingers like sand, and she was always knocking on the door begging a jar of coffee and this and that. She was also funny, kind and loyal, and the two were good friends.

Melody decided she had to tell Caroline who her date was. The other girl's reaction was pretty much as she had expected and mirrored her mother's earlier anxiety—if expressed somewhat differently.

'Not Mr Zipper himself?' Caroline groaned. 'What line did he give you this time?' And without giving Melody a chance to answer, she continued, 'I bet it was all hearts and roses with maybe a diamond or two thrown in? You can't fool for it, Melody, you just can't.'

'It wasn't like that.'

'It's always like that with his type,' Caroline said firmly. 'They think all they have to do is to arrive suitably penitent and little-boyish and you'll fall into their arms.'

'I contacted him,' Melody said in a rush—the only way she could get a word in edgeways. The statement struck Caroline dumb, which enabled Melody to add, 'About a case I wanted him to take on.'

Caroline frowned her disbelief.

'Really,' Melody insisted. 'My mother's in an awful fix through no fault of her own and I asked Zeke to help. He's terribly good at what he does.'

Caroline's eyebrows rose. 'That's never been in dispute,' she drawled. 'Only that he confines what he does to you.'

'It's not like that,' Melody said again, her voice little more than a whisper as she glanced anxiously along the landing to her closed front door. She didn't want Zeke hearing any of this. 'He's agreed to take the case and we are just seeing each other as friends now. That's all.'

Caroline grimaced, curling her lip in a way that did away with the need for words.

'Honestly.' Melody hesitated. 'He…well, Zeke's made it clear he doesn't want to pick up where we left off. He's not looking for a relationship with anyone at the moment and I'd be at the bottom of the list anyway.'

Caroline stared at her. 'Is that what he's said? Babe, six months ago the guy was crazy about you, even if he couldn't resist the male-ego thing of having his cake and eating it. Don't tell me a red-blooded zipper man like Zeke has gone all platonic on you 'cos I don't believe it.'

'I don't think he did. Have his cake and eat it, I mean.' Melody's voice was small. 'I was wrong about the thing with the secretary.'

'I *knew* it!' Caroline's voice was too loud and Melody winced, glancing at her door again. Thankfully it remained shut.

'I knew he'd talk you round at some point,' Caroline continued. 'You're just too nice, that's the trouble. Mel, the guy broke your heart; have you forgotten that?' she asked in a furious whisper as Melody tried to shush her. 'Now, listen to me…' She took hold of Melody's arm and drew her back inside the bathroom, shutting the door before she said, 'What he's done once, he'll do again. They always do if they're that type.'

'He's not.' Melody stared at her helplessly. 'He's not that type but I've realised it too late. I think I really hurt him when I accused him of the affair with Angela.'

'Hurt him or injured his pride?' Caroline asked caustically. 'Or maybe it was simply that he didn't like being caught out for once.'

Melody shook her head. 'We went out to dinner last night—' Caroline groaned but Melody ignored it '—and he put his side of things. I believed him. He also stated any future for us is not on the cards.'

'So why has he turned up tonight?'

'He needed a partner for a party his friend's throwing.'

'Hmph!'

'Look, I have to go.' Melody touched her friend's arm, her voice soft as she said, 'Thanks for caring but you're wrong about Zeke. *I* was wrong about Zeke. I misled you. You did like him once, remember?'

'Mel, there isn't a woman alive who wouldn't like Zeke if he put his mind to charming her,' Caroline said drily. 'He can be irresistible, I'll give you that, but it would take more than a talk over dinner to convince me he wasn't having trouble with his zipper again. But if you're absolutely convinced it's all over between you…'

'I am,' Melody said definitely.

'Then I don't suppose I've got anything to worry about,' Caroline said—worriedly. 'Look, Juan will be gone tomorrow—and don't laugh; that *is* his real name but without the Don in front of it…he's Spanish—so come and have a coffee with me. OK? We can have a girly chat.'

Melody tried to look enthusiastic when she said, 'Lovely; about eleven?'

Zeke was flipping through a wildlife magazine—sent by a charity she supported—when Melody entered the bedsit again. He glanced up as she walked into the room, the tawny gaze revealing nothing.

'I'm sorry I've kept you waiting,' she said as evenly as her breathing would allow. It annoyed her that her stomach had done a somersault at the sight of him but he'd always had that sort of effect on her. Her and the whole female sex, she added ruefully.

'No problem.'

He didn't smile but continued looking at her, and she found she was all fingers and thumbs as she collected her bag and light summer jacket. He looked dark and brooding and devastatingly sexy, and as she'd done a hundred times in the past she found herself wondering what it would be like for a woman to lose her virginity to a virile, experienced man like Zeke. What it would be like for *her*. But she'd never know now. And it was all her own fault.

'Did you call Brad to let him know you were bringing me along?' she asked as he stood up and walked over to the door, speaking mainly to keep her mind from wandering down forbidden avenues.

'No.'

As she locked the bedsit door Melody was acutely aware of him standing just behind her. He wasn't touching her but the height and breadth of him seemed to encompass her and she knew she was all of a dither. She tried to force herself to project an air of cool composure but her hot cheeks and shaking hands wouldn't obey her head.

As she turned to face him, he said, 'I thought we'd surprise everyone.'

Great. Well, the pair of them were guaranteed an entrance if nothing else. This was doubly unsettling, considering Brad and the rest of Zeke's crowd almost certainly would regard her as public enemy number one after the way she'd broken off their engagement. 'Perhaps horrify would be more appropriate?' she said with an attempt at nonchalance that didn't quite come off. 'They must all hate me.'

His eyes were golden, unblinking, his firm mouth twisted in a cynical smile. 'Do you really care what Brad or any of the others think of you?' he asked softly.

She stared at him. He must think she was as hard as nails. 'Yes, actually.'

'Rest assured, even Brad knows better than to say a word to upset you. Whatever their private thoughts when they see us together, everyone will be polite. They know I wouldn't tolerate anything less.'

Did he really think that was comforting? A sudden dart of anger at the situation he'd purposely put her in made her voice sharp when she said, 'I'll look forward to a wonderful evening, then.'

'As shall I,' murmured Zeke.

Melody's muscles clenched. He was playing with her, like a cat with a mouse, but there was nothing she could do. She'd tried telling him she believed she'd been wrong but he wouldn't accept she meant it, and she wasn't about to get down on bended knee and beg.

She wasn't aware of straightening her shoulders or the way her chin lifted, but the subtle body language wasn't missed on the big man watching her so closely.

As they turned and made their way downstairs, Zeke found himself confessing to reluctant admiration. She'd got guts, he'd give her that, he thought, his stomach twisting as he caught a whiff of the exotic, sensuous perfume she was wearing. But then he'd never doubted it. It was one of the qualities which had made him fall in love with her in the first place. That and her warmth, her gentleness, her strength, her beauty...

He caught the way his mind was going, ruthlessly reminding himself that her softness hid a determination that could be as inflexible as steel on occasion. The furious, blazing-eyed woman who had confronted him that day six months ago had been as soft as an armoured tank, and just as prepared to listen to reason.

He took her arm as they reached the entrance hall and exited the house, the silky feel of her skin and the way the smooth curtain of her hair brushed the rounded curves of her shoulders causing his loins to tighten. He was no longer exactly sure where all this was going and what it was he wanted from her, but whatever it was, he knew retribution only played a small part in it.

CHAPTER FIVE

By THE time they got to the party Melody was as tense as piano wire. She had steeled herself for the moment when Zeke slid into the car beside her, but nevertheless, the overt proximity of his large male body in the close confines of the powerful sports car was disconcerting—to say the least.

Brad had a flamboyant bachelor pad in a street close to the Strand and she had been there before on numerous occasions when she and Zeke had still been together, but now as Zeke helped her out of the car she noticed a 'Sold' sign with some surprise. 'That's not Brad's place, is it?' she asked as they crossed the pavement. 'He's not moving?' The house had been converted into two large apartments some years before, Brad owning the bottom one, which consisted of a lower and ground floor, and another staunch bachelor owning the top two floors. The parties they both threw were legendary.

Zeke nodded as he rang the doorbell. 'He's moving to a house in Streatham in a couple of weeks.'

Melody stared at him, utterly amazed. 'He's leaving the apartment? But he absolutely loves it here. Why is he moving?'

'His fiancée didn't want to start their married life in a

place which has seen more than a few women come and go over the years,' Zeke said drily.

'His *fiancée*?' When she had left Zeke six months before Brad had still been a confirmed love-'em-and-leave-'em ladies' man to whom settling down with one woman would be anathema.

Zeke's lips twitched at her blatant surprise. 'He met Kate a couple of weeks after we split and it was the proverbial love at first sight—on both sides. At thirty-five and thirty-seven respectively they didn't want to waste any more time. Kate's biological clock went into overdrive as soon as she laid eyes on Brad and he's up for a family—hence the move to the traditional three-bedroomed house, where they hope the 2.4 kids will soon follow.'

Melody became aware her mouth was open and shut it with a little snap. She would have sworn on oath that she was certain Brad would remain a bachelor until his dying day. She said weakly, 'But he loved the apartment.'

'He loves Kate more.'

And then the door opened and there stood Brad with his arm round a tall, willowy brunette whom Melody took to be Kate. She had it in her to feel sorry for Zeke's best friend. At least she'd had a little warning about Kate, but from the look on Brad's face he hadn't had a clue that she was back in Zeke's life—albeit temporarily.

Brad recovered magnificently. 'Melody, what a surprise.' His eyes had flashed to Zeke's impassive face and then back to hers. 'You haven't met Kate, have you? Kate, this is Melody. She...' He floundered for a moment.

'I'm a friend of Zeke's.' Melody reached out and shook the hand the other woman proffered. She could tell Brad had spoken of her in the past because his fiancée's eyes had widened at her name. '*Just* a friend,' she added, mainly for

Brad's benefit so he didn't get the wrong idea, but also to make a point to Zeke. Quite what point she was making she wasn't sure, she just knew there was one to be made.

'Come and have a drink.' Kate reached out to her and swept her into the throng inside, leaving the two men to follow. Melody could have kissed the other woman for making a bad moment a little easier. Kate kept her arm linked through Melody's as they walked over to the bar in the lounge. This bar was Brad's pride and joy and as well-stocked as any pub.

Melody asked for a glass of red wine and, once Kate had handed her one, the other woman said, 'Brad's going to miss this more than anything else, I think. He loves to show off at parties and this bar is his pièce de résistance.'

'He could have one in the new house,' Melody offered tentatively, appreciating that Kate hadn't abandoned her once she had the drink. Neither was she asking awkward questions.

'Over my dead body.' Kate grinned at her. 'He has the makings of a good family man but the less temptation the better.'

Melody smiled weakly back. 'Did you have a place to sell?' she asked, not because she really wanted to know but to keep the conversation going. She was aware of more than a few glances in her direction and hadn't missed the way the hubbub had quietened for a few moments when she'd walked in.

Kate nodded. 'Tiny one-bedroomed flat; nothing like this. It sold in twenty-four hours. I'm staying with a girl-friend until the wedding. I wouldn't stay here if you paid me in diamonds.'

Melody could understand that. 'When is the wedding?'

'Didn't Zeke tell you?' The two men had just reached them and now Kate said, 'Zeke, do you mean to tell me you haven't invited Melody to the wedding? You must come, Melody. It's totally informal. We're marrying on a boat on the Thames in two weeks' time—it'll be such fun. Zeke's best man and my sister is giving me away. My dog is the only bridesmaid; she's a little cocker spaniel and we've got her the cutest little lace coat.'

Melody glanced at Brad and saw he had an inane grin on his handsome face. He also couldn't keep his eyes off Kate. He really *was* smitten, Melody thought in amazement. And yet Kate wasn't his normal type of woman at all. He'd always gone for petite blondes in the past, preferably ones with over-developed mammary glands. Kate was tall and slender with a boyish figure and an attractive—rather than pretty—face.

Zeke took her arm, causing a hundred nerves to jangle as he drew her into his side with a casual air. 'That's not a bad idea, Kate,' he drawled lazily. 'I know the best man usually partners the bridesmaid but, as cute as Muffin's bound to look in her lace coat, I'd rather dance the night away with Melody. What do you think, Melody?' he added, glancing down at her with a wicked glint in his eyes. 'Fancy partnering an old friend for the day?'

He expected her to decline and make some excuse; she could read it in his face. Melody felt herself go pink as the three of them looked at her. She was vitally aware of his hand on her arm and the feel of his muscled thigh as he held her against him, the scent of his aftershave—a mixture of lime and something sexy—doing the strangest things to her heartbeat. For a moment the urge to smack the mockery off his face was so strong she could taste it.

He thought he had her weighed up and it was galling, the more so because her first impulse had been to do exactly what he expected and politely refuse the invitation.

She felt cornered. Then she found herself saying brightly, 'I'd love to come, Kate. You must let me have your wedding list before then.'

'Oh, don't worry about that.' Kate looked delighted and Brad looked bemused. 'Zeke's already gone overboard and paid for our honeymoon—ten days in Venice.'

'What can you get the couple who have got everything?' Zeke interjected smoothly.

'I'd still like the list,' Melody said firmly, keeping her smile in place with some effort. 'I wouldn't feel comfortable if I didn't get you something myself; I'm sure you understand.'

Again Kate came through for her.

'Absolutely,' the other woman said easily, linking her arm through Brad's. 'I'd be just the same. But we haven't actually got a list—everything's been too quick! Just surprise us with a little something and that will be lovely. We've got a nice garden where we're going and no gardening tools whatsoever, if that gives you any ideas. If you don't mind buying something practical…?'

'Not at all.' Melody smiled. 'I'd hate you to end up with twenty vases or a stack of fruit bowls.'

Kate continued talking about their new house for a while and Melody responded as naturally as she could, but inside a weight of sadness had settled on her. She and Zeke had talked of buying a house somewhere on the outskirts of London in the future, but initially she had agreed to move into his spacious three-bedroomed apartment close to his work when they married. She hadn't had any reservations about that, she'd just wanted to be with him and had agreed it would be fun to house-hunt as an old married couple. Seeing Kate's transparent happiness was bringing back so many deeply emotional memories she'd tried to shut out of her mind for the last six months.

Eventually Kate and Brad moved away to circulate amongst their other guests. Melody turned to Zeke, her voice quiet when she said, 'Brad's changed.'

'For the better?' he asked softly, one dark brow raised.

She nodded. 'I think so. Kate's going to be very good for him.'

'And he for her hopefully.'

She nodded again but said nothing. She couldn't. She was too terrified she'd disgrace herself by bursting into tears.

'You've changed too,' he said after a moment or two.

She took a deep breath and banished any tears by sheer will-power. 'Good or bad?' she asked with what she hoped was a light tone. She didn't want him to suspect how important his opinion was to her.

He took a sip of wine before he replied and then his voice was without expression. 'Both, I guess.'

She looked him full in the face and found the amber eyes were waiting for her. 'How exactly?' She didn't really want to know but she had to ask nevertheless.

'You seem more sure of yourself than I remember,' he said slowly. 'And that's good. I noticed it at the house with your mother and several times since.'

She didn't like to tell him he was completely wrong and that she'd never felt less sure of herself or anything else for that matter since he'd come back into her life. 'Perhaps it's the new job,' she said carefully. 'It carries more responsibility.'

He inclined his head, finishing the glass of wine before he said, 'Maybe.'

She stared at him. 'And the bad?'

He paused for a second and then shrugged. 'Forget it,' he said quietly.

'I'd like to know.' She ignored the sick churning in her stomach. 'You can't say something like that and then not follow through.'

She saw him take a deep breath and then he seemed to pick his words carefully when he said, 'You seem more reserved, less…warm. As though something's missing.'

He had turned away to gaze over the room as he spoke and she was glad of it. She stared at the rugged profile, her mind screaming, You! It's you that's missing. Can't you see that? She tried to keep her voice even and flat when she said, 'It's been a tough six months,' but it must have wobbled a little because the tawny gaze shot to her face again.

'With your work, you mean?'

Blow my work. 'Not altogether.' She couldn't do this. She *really* couldn't do this. She took a great gulp of wine and held out her empty glass. 'I need to go to the cloakroom. I'll be back in a minute.'

He seemed nonplussed for a second at the suddenness of her announcement, recovering almost instantly to say, 'Same again?'

'Please.' And then she turned on her heel and all but ran for the safety of Brad's little cloakroom off the hall.

So what did all that mean? Zeke stood gazing after Melody for a good few seconds after she'd disappeared. Had she missed him? Was that what she'd been hinting at? If she had, it hadn't been enough to contact him or even offer to talk things through and let him present his side of things.

He walked across to the bar and refilled both their glasses before finding a quiet corner by a window and turning his back on the room and its inhabitants. When he thought of how they'd confided in each other before the split, woven dreams for their future, spoken all their hopes and fears. At least *he* had. He frowned to himself. He'd always sensed he wasn't getting all of Melody but he had thought that would change once they were married, once he could fully prove to her just how much he loved her, how much she meant to him.

In spite of the fact that she had chosen a demanding and often exhausting profession, she had always seemed infinitely fragile to him. He'd wanted to protect her, to stand guard over her so no one could hurt her... He shook his head at himself, annoyed with the way his thoughts were going. Which was probably why he'd felt such a jerk when she had shown him she didn't need him at all. She had been able to walk away from him and not look back, and deep inside he knew, whatever she might have done to him, however bad the betrayal, he wouldn't have been able to let her go. *Damn it.* His mouth hardened into a thin line. Whatever poet had said that love made fools of men had got it right.

She was so distant with him now. He turned round and surveyed the room, his dark, brooding persona making sure no one made the mistake of trying to engage him in conversation. And yet she wasn't like that with anyone else. Look at Kate—the two of them had hit it off immediately, and he knew Melody's intrinsic tenderness enabled her to be damned good at her job. She had that way of getting people to relax and open up to her.

How could she think he would sleep with another woman when he was committed to her? His stomach writhed.

She had said she didn't believe that any more, a little voice at the back of his mind reminded him.

Did he believe that? No. Not for a moment. When they

had stood outside her mother's house and again at dinner last night her face—as well as her words—had confirmed her contempt for him.

He tried to deliberately blank his mind. This was a party, for crying out loud, Brad's farewell to this flat and his embracing of a new life and new home. It wasn't the time for morbid reflections.

He could still catch Melody on the raw. His eyes swept the room but he wasn't seeing anyone. But it wasn't giving him any satisfaction. The trouble was this attraction she held for him wouldn't die a death and was still uppermost. He had been trying to ignore the way he felt and keep a tight lid on his feelings but she got to him. It was galling— incredibly galling—to admit, but she got to him in a way he knew no other woman would ever do again.

He had always despised men who allowed their woman to walk all over them. *But here he was, in danger of doing just that.*

No, no, he wasn't. He stiffened, muscles taut. And Melody wasn't his woman anyway, not any more. So what was she to him? A friend, as he'd suggested to her? His lips curved cynically. Ludicrous.

'There's a six-foot aura around you that is as black as the ace of spaces and is scaring my guests to death.'

Brad's voice brought Zeke out of his thoughts, his eyes focusing on the other man with something like astonishment in their amber depths. In truth he'd been so immersed in his dark thoughts the room and the people in it had ceased to exist.

'Couldn't be anything to do with your date, could it?' Brad continued drily. 'So when did you two meet up again?'

Zeke smiled but it didn't reach his eyes. 'Don't put two and two together and make ten. Melody asked me to represent her mother, that's all. Anna's in a spot of bother through no fault of her own so I said I'd oblige.'

'That's very magnanimous of you, considering your history with the wicked witch of the west,' said Brad, his eyebrows rising. 'I'd have thought you'd take great pleasure in seeing her squirm.'

Melody reappeared across the room at that moment, and as Zeke glanced at her Brad looked from him to her. 'Ah, I see,' he muttered half to himself.

'What do you think you see?' Zeke asked irritably. 'No—' he held out his hand as Brad went to reply '—on second thoughts, I don't want to know. But whatever it is, you're barking up the wrong tree. There's nothing between Melody and myself now, except perhaps friendship.'

Even as he spoke, Zeke knew his friend wouldn't believe him. They had known each other too long not to know when the other one wasn't being completely honest.

Melody reached them in the next instant, accepting the glass of wine Zeke gave her with a smile of thanks before she engaged Brad in conversation ostensibly about his forthcoming marriage. Other folk joined them in the next few minutes and soon there was a group of the old crowd.

Melody was surprised how easy it was to be with everyone—everyone except one particular person anyway. She was careful to keep her gaze averted from Zeke but she was aware of every little movement he made, every turn of his head, every smile. He was more relaxed than when they'd first arrived, his face animated and even a little boyish as he argued with one of his friends about the merits of different football teams. He looked good enough to eat.

The rest of the evening passed fairly well, mainly because they were never alone. Melody was conscious that she was watching Zeke most of the time but she couldn't help it. She was also aware that a good few other females were watching him too, but that was nothing out of the ordinary. It had always been like that from the day she'd met him. It was something she realised she'd never got used to, though. Not that he'd ever responded to other women's smiles and come-ons, she admitted silently, but they had rankled nevertheless.

It was gone two by the time they left the apartment. At some point during the proceedings Melody had found herself promising to look after Kate's dog, Muffin, on the big day should the need present itself. 'My mother's having her while we're in Venice,' Kate had explained, 'but she wants to do the mother-of-the-bride thing with a snazzy outfit and big hat on the day. She's hugely disappointed it's not a top-hat-and-tails affair in a church with all the trimmings, so I don't dare ask her to take charge of Muffin for the day. You probably won't need to do a thing, she's such a good dog, but just in case she gets too excited or something it would be good to know someone is looking out for her.'

Once in Zeke's car, Melody leant back in the seat with a sigh. How had she come to agree to attend a wedding where Zeke was best man and she was looking after the bride's pet dog?

'What's the matter?' Zeke glanced at her as he turned the key in the ignition, the powerful car purring in obedience.

'Nothing.' Melody was acutely aware Zeke had only had one glass of wine before going on to mineral water because he was driving, whereas she had recklessly downed several glasses of a somewhat lethal red. It put her at a definite disadvantage because any alcohol always made her tongue run away with itself. Hence her agreement to dogsit Muffin. But consenting to look after a dog was one thing; what she might reveal to Zeke in an unguarded moment was quite another. It was bad enough that he had dismissed her attempt to tell him she'd been wrong about him and Angela earlier; she'd just die if he suspected she wanted him to kiss her. But she did. So much.

'You seemed to be enjoying yourself back there.'

Melody glanced at him out of the corner of her eye. He was wearing a light blue shirt and no tie, the top couple of buttons undone just enough to expose the dark shadow of chest hair, and his charcoal trousers pulled tight over lean, muscled thighs in the limited confines of the car. She was glad she was sitting down because he made her knees weak. She had to moisten dry lips before she could say, 'It was very nice.'

This wasn't quite true. If they had been a couple again it would have been a wonderful, an incredible evening, as any evening had been with him. As it was, she had felt such a mixture of emotions all evening she felt quite exhausted. As well as horribly sexually frustrated, she admitted wryly. Zeke, on the other hand, was the epitome of cool control, an enigmatic stranger, in fact.

Melody wriggled in her seat. He had kissed her on her mother's doorstep but hadn't seemed bothered enough to try again. Had that kiss been enough to tell him he didn't have the slightest interest in her any more—in *that* way? It was funny; she'd had all these ideas she was going to have to fight him off and instead he didn't want to know.

Why didn't he fancy her any more? She hadn't grown two heads or developed a problem with body odour. What was putting him off?

She glanced at him again, feeling extremely miffed, but then in the next instant the pique was swept away as the enormity of what she'd lost engulfed her. She'd been such a fool. She would give the world to go back in time before she left him. She shivered slightly although the night was a warm, balmy one and she was wearing her linen jacket.

'Cold?' Zeke turned up the heating. 'It's the change of atmosphere.'

No, it's because you don't want me any more. She burrowed into her seat, suddenly feeling very small and very alone. The need to try and convince him that she knew she'd been terribly wrong was almost overpowering, but the way he had dismissed her earlier attempt told her he wouldn't believe her.

'I'm going to try and settle your mother's case before it goes as far as coming to court—did she tell you?' Zeke asked after they had driven some way in silence.

Melody was so tense she had jumped as he'd spoken, and it took a moment for her to be able to say, 'No, she didn't.'

'After looking at all the papers I'd say the opposition have got a damn good argument, but they might see reason. A little bluff can go a long way on occasion,' he said drily. 'Anyway, we're discussing all the pros and cons over Sunday lunch before we go ahead and approach the other solicitor.'

You're having lunch with my mother?' She stared at him, wide-eyed. She'd never—not in her wildest dreams—thought to see such a day.

'A business lunch,' he corrected evenly. 'I've got a manic week in store and Sunday was the only time I could see her. It was your mother who suggested lunch,' he added expressionlessly.

Shock was replaced by foreboding. Was her mother intending to quiz Zeke about their relationship under cover of discussing business?

'Don't look so worried,' Zeke said with a touch of

amusement in his voice. 'I dare say we'll both survive the experience of seeing each other without you to deflect any arrows. Who knows, we might actually find we can tolerate each other?' The look on his face belied this.

'She…she might be awkward,' Melody warned weakly.

'Not if she wants me to stay, she won't.' It was very definite. 'I don't have to take any—' He stopped abruptly, and when he continued, 'Rubbish,' Melody knew he'd been about to say a stronger word. 'For once she'll toe the line or else.'

This had all the makings of a disaster. 'Zeke, my father hurt her very badly when he left. She's damaged—'

'And she in turn damaged you pretty thoroughly.' His voice wasn't confrontational or loud but it possessed a quality which brought Melody's mouth tightening. 'Which in my book is inexcusable. OK, so the man was something that crawled out from under a stone, I can see that. The way he's never tried to see you is proof enough. But only so much can be laid at his door, Melody. She's fed you a diet of insecurity and distrust against the whole male sex from when you could walk, and that was *her* doing. Not his.'

'How can you say that?' She was enraged. 'He was terrible to her—'

'I'm not saying he wasn't or that she didn't have a hell of a lot to put up with,' he interrupted grimly. 'But that still doesn't negate feeding you poison.'

'You don't know that,' she said furiously. 'You weren't there, for goodness' sake.'

'Goodness has nothing to do with it and I know it all right. I've reaped the result.'

'You've never liked my mother,' she accused hotly.

'Dead right.' He flashed her one glance from scorching eyes. 'I'd as soon get pally with a boa constrictor. But I *was* prepared to keep things amicable and get along with her for your sake. Unfortunately she didn't show me the same courtesy. But that's in the past. None of it matters now.

It felt as if he'd just punched her in the chest. Melody swallowed hard.

'She's done too thorough a job on you, can't you see that?' he said roughly. 'Damn it, woman, wake up before you throw your life away and become a carbon copy of her.'

'You don't understand.' She was fighting very hard not to cry. 'Beneath the outward façade you can see she's still so vulnerable. I know she was wrong to do what she did.' She swallowed again against the huge lump in her throat. 'But she misguidedly thought she was doing the best for me. She really believed you were playing around with Angela.'

'So did you,' he reminded her grimly.

Her chin went up a notch. 'Yes, I did, and I'm more sorry than words can say that I didn't trust you more.' Funnily enough it was easy to say now the moment had arrived. 'I let you down and ruined everything between us and I can't make that right. The only thing I can do is to tell you now that I know I was wrong, however the photographs looked.'

There was a deep, deep silence for a moment. Then he said, 'What's changed your mind?'

She had to answer honestly. 'I don't know,' she admitted wearily. 'I wish I did. But suddenly last night it just seemed impossible you could do something like that.'

Silence reigned again. The car sped on through streets devoid of heavy traffic but still busy enough.

When they eventually came to a stop outside the house where the bedsit was, the atmosphere in the car was so tense it was crackling. Melody was gripping her handbag so hard her knuckles were white.

Zeke turned off the engine and the quiet of a city night descended, the background noise of minor traffic barely impinging inside the car.

She didn't move. She couldn't move. And she had no idea what he would do or say next. She just knew she had nothing left to say.

Eventually he stirred. 'I've missed you,' he said thickly. 'So much.' *And I still love you. I know I'll always love you. All the garbage I've told myself over the last six months about getting over you is just that—garbage. The minute I had a chance to have you back in my life, for whatever reason, I took it. Which makes me the biggest fool going.* 'But I don't know if I can do this again. Do us again.'

'I know I don't deserve to be forgiven—'

'It's not that.' He made a swift downward motion with his hand, cutting off her voice. 'Believe me, it's not that. But I'm not sure we wouldn't go through the same thing again. You torture yourself—' He stopped abruptly.

Melody watched the big tom from several doors up saunter along the pavement, tail erect and head held at a jaunty angle. Not a care in the world, she thought, envying the cat with all her heart.

'I'm not the kind of guy to pussyfoot about, Melody,' Zeke said grimly. 'To forever be looking over my shoulder, wondering if I've crossed the line in some scenario you're playing out in your mind. And this isn't just about Angela. We both know that. Long before that, from when we first met, you were waiting for me to fail you. You've never trusted me. That's the bottom line.'

She couldn't deny it because she knew it to be the truth. She said the only thing she could. 'I'm sorry.'

'It was tough losing my mum and dad.' His voice was

quiet now, controlled. 'But worse losing you. But you didn't feel like that—'

'I did, oh, I did.' She turned to him, grasping his arm. 'I nearly went mad. I couldn't eat, couldn't sleep—'

'But you didn't come back to me.'

'No.' She let her hand fall limply away.

'Because you were so sure I'd been having an affair. And it was that same thinking that always made you keep a little bit of yourself where I couldn't reach you.'

'So.' He was the first to break the charged silence after a full minute had ticked endlessly away. 'Where do we go from here?'

She didn't answer. He watched her tongue slide nervously across her lower lip, leaving it damp with moisture. Every nerve in his body responded.

'Do we go back to the beginning?' he asked very softly. 'Start seeing each other again? Taking it slowly, a day at a time? Nothing heavy, no promises. Just seeing where it goes?'

It was more than she had ever expected. Melody lifted her eyes. 'Yes, please,' she whispered.

'But this time we talk,' he warned steadily. 'No jumping to conclusions, no secret worries, no listening to other people. I'm your first port of call and you are mine. Even if I don't like what you say, you say it to me and I'll take it on the chin and appreciate what it's costing you to come out in the open. Can you live with that?'

She nodded.

'I'm being honest with you here, Melody. I don't know if love is enough for us but I can't walk away from you right now. I don't want to. I never have. I want it to work but sometimes wanting isn't enough, I realise that now. But we can give it our best shot and see where it goes.'

She nodded again, tears of relief, of pain, of aching hunger spilling from her eyes.

It was all he needed. Zeke lowered his head and took her mouth, pulling her into him as he tasted the sweetness that he remembered. He didn't want to talk or discuss or rationalise any more. He just wanted to hold her in his arms and feel her against him.

She responded immediately, her mouth eager against his inviting tongue in the dark shadows within the car, her body shaping itself to his as he curved over her and as the kiss became more passionate. He groaned deep in his throat, catching her hair in his fingers as he pulled her even closer.

Her hands had slid up to his shoulders as she clasped him to her, tremors coursing through her body as his touch moved to her breasts. His big hands cupped their fullness through the thin material covering them and she shivered violently.

He moved slightly, his fingers returning to her hair as he deepened the kiss until a small moan escaped her lips. The feel of her firm breasts against his chest was the most heady of aphrodisiacs and now it was taking all his self-control to keep his passion in check. After all, they were in a car in the street, where anyone could see them.

'I've burned for you…' His voice was husky against her mouth, desire racing through his bloodstream, igniting nerve-endings and arousing him more and more. He moved his hips and her softness moulded into his hardness like a human jigsaw. It was exquisite torture. 'Night after night I've burned for you.'

The sound of a car engine turning into the top of the street registered in his consciousness but for a moment he couldn't respond. Then he dragged his mouth from hers, drawing in a gasp of air as though he'd been swimming under water for minutes.

Melody's eyes were closed. She opened them slowly, bewilderedly, as though she was dazed, and it was only when he gently adjusted her clothing and moved into his own seat that she became aware of the taxi drawing to a halt just a few yards away, its headlights bright in the darkness. Two couples noisily emerged and by the time one of the men had paid the cab driver, the others stumbling about on the pavement and calling ribald remarks to each other, sanity had been restored.

Zeke's mouth had curved into a crooked smile. 'Saved by the bell, or in this case your neighbours,' he said drily, opening his car door and walking round the bonnet of the car to her. Melody watched him in the shadowed night. She still couldn't quite believe this was happening. The cool, controlled stranger of the last couple of days had gone and in his place was the Zeke she'd known before. And yet... not quite.

He opened the door for her, helping her out with the old-fashioned American charm she'd found so delightful when they had first begun dating. He'd been brought up in Texas until the age of twenty-one, he'd told her, and there men were still men and women were still women, and both sexes liked it that way.

'I'll see you to your door.' He had taken her in his arms again as she'd exited the car and kissed her very thoroughly, and now she emerged breathless and flushed from his embrace.

'All right.' Would he want to come in? She hoped so. Even though—with the fire burning so fiercely between them—it was dangerous. But she wanted him. Oh, how she wanted him. The separation of the last months had caused a need that was unquenchable with just kisses and caressing.

They walked hand in hand into the house and Melody

felt as though she was floating. She wanted to laugh out loud on the one hand and burst into tears of sheer emotion on the other. She did neither, stopping outside her door and lifting her face to him. 'Would you like to come in?' she asked shyly.

Zeke was looking at her in a way she couldn't quite fathom. An intense, searching look. 'I'd like to but I won't,' he said very softly.

'Why?'

'Because I can't trust myself tonight.'

She stared at him, her heart pounding at what she was going to say next. 'Maybe I don't want you to.' He looked very big and dark and heart-wrenchingly handsome, and the wonder that she had been given a second chance of sorts had her light-headed.

'Then that's double the reason to say no.'

It wasn't what she'd expected him to say and her face revealed this, even before she said, her voice small, 'I see.'

'No, you don't.' He lifted her chin so she had to stare into his face. 'Melody, when I met you I couldn't believe you were still a virgin, not looking like you do and being so sweet, so warm…' He paused, taking control of himself before he continued, 'You were fresh and innocent in a world that's anything but. Not childlike—hell, no,' he said ruefully, 'you're all woman, but there was a gentleness about you. And I liked your dream. Of wearing white and it meaning something. Even though it caused me one hell of a problem that countless cold showers didn't even begin to touch.'

He kissed her, hard.

'I'd had women, but you know that. Some I had to wait for—for a week or a month; others…I didn't. But you were special. *We* were special. For the first time I could envisage sharing my life with someone, of having kids.

You would be the mother of my children.' He stopped, shaking his head. 'I'm not explaining this very well. But it was right at the time. Right that we waited.'

'And now?' she asked, something in his voice making her feel the way she had in the car. This was the old Zeke and yet…not. There was a reserve about him, a restraint. Something.

'Now nothing is so straightforward,' he said gently. 'We've come a long way tonight but you know as well as I do that this is going to take time. Whatever happens I don't want to confuse things.'

She stared at him, her eyes dominating her entire face in the subdued light on the landing. She felt all at sea. And let down. And yet she shouldn't. But she did. 'I see,' she said again. 'Well, if that's how you feel…' She couldn't go on.

He looked as though he was about to say more but instead he took a physical step backwards, his voice very controlled when he said, 'Goodnight, Melody.'

'Goodnight.' Don't go. Stay. Let me convince you I love you more than life itself. That I'll never let you down again. That I'll trust you whatever happens.

When she heard the front door to the house close Melody was still standing exactly where Zeke had left her, one hand clutching her throat and the other against her chest. She stood there for a few moments more before glancing along the landing towards Caroline's room.

How was she going to explain the fact that she and Zeke were back together to Caroline? she thought dazedly, let alone all the ifs and buts that went with it. Caroline was such a free spirit without an intense bone in her body, and her lifestyle was the very antithesis to the other woman's. Caroline would have bedded Zeke before he could blink and taken enormous pleasure over the experience too. No hang-ups. No worries. No inhibitions.

She turned, opening the door of the bedsit and stepping inside, where she continued to stand in the darkness.

Caroline would think she was absolutely crazy.

CHAPTER SIX

AS IT happened, Caroline surprised her.

It might have been because—after a virtually sleepless night when Melody had dissected every word, every look, every gesture of Zeke's until her brain was buzzing—she looked dreadful. Certainly when Caroline opened the door to her tentative knock her eyes widened in concern, and the expletive that followed against Zeke was very explicit.

'I knew it.' Caroline hauled her into the bedsit and sat her down on the sofa before Melody could say a word. 'I just knew he'd break your heart again. What happened? He's playing fast and loose, isn't he? The swine. They're all the same, these drop-dead gorgeous ones.'

'You've got it wrong—'

'You just give me his telephone number and I'll tell him what's what, the creep.'

Caroline.' Melody seldom raised her voice, so it had the required effect when she did. 'Everything is fine. He was great. Just great.'

'So why do you look like death warmed up?' said Caroline, never one to mince her words.

'It's a long story.'

'I've got the whole day.' Caroline leapt up from her

position at Melody's side and shot over to the coffee-pot, pouring them both a mug before bringing the tray—on which reposed two wicked chocolate muffins along with the coffee—over to the sofa. She accomplished the whole procedure in twenty seconds flat. 'So, what gives?' she said, plonking herself down beside Melody. 'Tell all to your personal confessor and I'll give you the benefit of my years of surviving in a man's world.'

Melody couldn't help grinning. It might be a man's world but Caroline had long since perfected the art of making any males within her sphere dance to her tune.

Several cups of coffee and two chocolate muffins each later, Caroline licked sticky fingers before she said, 'So basically Zeke's whiter than white and the two of you are back on—sort of,' she qualified thoughtfully.

Melody nodded.

'OK, I'll buy it for the moment. But don't overdo the guilt thing too much, babe. Those photos were pretty hot and anyone would have jumped to the conclusion you did.'

'But someone else would have let him give his side of things before they dumped him.'

'Possibly, yeah.' Caroline sighed. 'But hindsight's a wonderful thing. I've gone for the jugular a few times only to find I was way off beam. None of us are perfect. And frankly I still think he's lucky to get you.'

Melody thought it was the other way round but her friend's unconditional support and affection was warming.

'And he's having lunch with your mother.' Caroline grimaced. 'If you take my advice you'd go and see her later and find out exactly what went on. Before you speak to Zeke again. And whatever she says, take it with a pinch of salt. When are you seeing him again anyway?'

'He didn't say.'

Caroline frowned. 'Playing it cool. Well, don't you dare act as though all you're waiting for is the phone to ring. You have a life outside Zeke Russell, OK? Be casual, don't agree to the first thing he suggests. Start making him hungry and he'll soon be at your beck and call.'

She didn't think she wanted him at her beck and call. She just wanted him.

Melody stared at the other girl and her face must have given her away because Caroline jumped to her feet, shaking her head as she said, 'You're a hopeless case. You know that, don't you? You're just too *nice* and you can't afford to be like that with men. I meant what I said—he *is* lucky to have you! Now, you're staying for lunch and no argument, and you're going to list some of the more yukky things about him to get him in perspective. Things like smelly feet and so on.'

Melody smiled, but she knew she wouldn't be able to think of a single one.

Mid-afternoon Melody arrived back in her own bedsit. She'd decided she was going to follow Caroline's suggestion and visit her mother. An hour later she let herself into her mother's house to find the older woman sitting in the lounge with a mass of papers strewn on the coffee-table in front of her.

'Hi.' She bent and gave the perfunctory kiss, which was all her mother ever allowed. 'How did the meeting with Zeke go?' She'd decided *en route* she wasn't going to beat about the bush.

Anna looked a little discomfited. 'Fine.'

'Good.' Melody waited for more and when nothing was forthcoming she said, 'Have you decided how you're going to proceed?' as she sat down in a big, comfy chair opposite Anna.

'Oh, yes.'

Melody arched an eyebrow. 'Care to let me in on the secret, then?' she asked patiently but with a slight edge to her voice to let her mother know she didn't appreciate the prevarication.

'Well, Zeke's managed to contact Julian and he's frightened him to death apparently. Hinted he'd got a couple of things on him which would look terribly bad if he waits until all this goes to court. He suggested Julian gets into the arena and comes clean. Of course, it won't let me off the hook but it might make negotiating more possible. Zeke's going to see the other lawyers and put everything to them once Julian's done his bit.'

'Right. And when will that be?'

'Tomorrow, I think, from how Zeke spoke.' Her mother put down the papers in her hand. 'Would you like some coffee?'

'Only if you're OK to stop. I don't have to stay.'

'No, of course, that's fine.' Her mother stood up abruptly, hightailing it into the kitchen in a way that wasn't like her cool, controlled manner at all.

Melody frowned. She stood up and followed Anna into the other room, leaning against the pale cream worktop and watching as her mother set a tray for two. 'What's the matter?' she asked quietly. 'Did you and Zeke row?'

'Row? Of course not. Whatever gave you that idea?' said Anna, as though the mere idea was preposterous.

'Then what is it?'

'What's what?'

Mother.' Melody took a deep breath and forced her voice down an octave or two. 'You're all on edge and you're never on edge.' Not visibly anyway. But she'd known from when she'd been a little girl that her mother lived on her nerves and the cool, icy front was just that—a front. 'So what's gone on I should know about?'

Anna stopped fiddling with the tray and turned, gazing at Melody with an expression that would have suggested helplessness in anyone else. But her mother was never helpless. Ever. 'Well?' Melody persisted.

'He… Zeke… I didn't…' Her mother waved her hands in an attitude that definitely had more than a touch of helplessness about it. 'We talked,' she managed at last. 'Not just about the case, but other things. He…he just isn't what I'd expected.'

Melody stared at her. 'In what way?' she asked carefully.

'Well, I expected that he wouldn't pull any punches—after all, we've never got on—and he *was* forthright, even blunt, but he wasn't so aggressive to me personally as I'd prepared myself for. In fact he was…'

'What?'

'Kind.'

Melody didn't know if she wanted to hug her mother or slap her. She took a deep breath. 'You might have found out what Zeke was like if you had been prepared to meet him properly in the past,' she said flatly. 'Instead it was always a fleeting couple of minutes here and there, and even then you managed to put his back up. How often did I tell you he wasn't like you thought? And all the times we asked you to have dinner with us or go out for a drink, anything.'

'I know.' Anna moved a saucer round the tray.

'So what did he say?'

'He insisted on clearing the air about the photographs straight away, and he let me know what he thought about my part in the proceedings.' Anna raised her gaze to that of her daughter's before dropping her eyes to the tray again. 'But he was so upfront and unconfrontational. He didn't try to manipulate or persuade me; he didn't even try to make me believe him. In fact he said yours was the only opinion that mattered to him. But he wanted me to know the facts because I…'

Again her mother faltered, and now Melody said, her interest heightened by the look on her mother's face, 'Because you what?'

'Because I was important to you. Because you loved me.'

Melody winced. There had been the slightest question mark in her mother's tone and it hurt more than she would have thought possible. She walked over to the older woman and did something she hadn't done in years—simply because her mother didn't like it—and put her arms round her, hugging her tight before kissing her on the mouth. 'Of course I love you,' she said very softly. 'I love you with all the world. Don't you know that?'

Anna tried to speak but she couldn't, the tears spilling out of her eyes and down her cheeks in an avalanche of pent-up emotion.

'Oh, Mum.' Melody found herself crying too and the coffee was forgotten as the two of them clung on to each other for a long time. Eventually they walked through to the lounge, sitting side by side on the sofa as they dried their eyes. 'Mum, you must know how important you are to me, surely?' Melody said, her voice tinged with amazement.

Anna dabbed at her eyes, shaking her head slightly as she said, 'But I've been such an awful mother, working all the hours under the sun and not spending much time with you. But I wanted to give you financial security; I didn't ever want us to be in the position we were in when your father left. That was such a terrible time and I can't forgive myself for how I was then. I've tried to always be strong for you since.'

'You have been.'

'After what I put you through then I promised myself I'd never be emotional again, not in front of you, to distress you. I owed you that.'

Melody wrinkled her brow. There was something here she was missing. 'You had every right to be upset,' she said quietly.

'But not to do what I did. I was out of my mind, that was the thing. The only good to come out of it was that it brought me to my senses. When I woke up in hospital and realised how close I'd come to dying, to leaving you all alone...' Anna wiped her eyes again. 'And then there was the fight with Social Services to convince them I was a fit mother and wouldn't do anything like it again.'

As her mother had spoken it was as though a light had been switched on in some dark corner of Melody's brain. The memory she'd buried for so long, the incident which had shaped her life without her consciously being aware of it was there in stark clarity. She could even smell the gas and see her mother lying on the floor in the kitchen with her head resting on a cushion propped in the stove; feel the bite of the neighbour's fingers as they'd jerked her away out into the hall and then fresh air. She had been nearly four years old and her mother had sent her to play with the neighbour's little girl for the afternoon. It had only been the fact that the other child had become nauseous after an hour or so that she had come home early...

'You tried to kill yourself.' She spoke the words as if in a dream.

'I was desperate,' her mother whispered brokenly. 'It's no excuse, I know, but there were unpaid bills, not a bite of food in the house.' She put her hand to her eyes. 'I had no idea where your father was but someone had said he'd left this other woman and gone off with a rich society girl abroad. It was the final straw.'

'And you were all alone.' Melody hugged her again and when her mother clung to her both of them were weeping again.

As though the floodgates had opened, memories and incidents were pouring in: a well-meaning friend of her mother's telling the four-year-old Melody she had to be a good girl and never worry her mother or else she would be ill again. She mustn't cry or call for her mother; she had to be very grown-up and always behave herself. And she must never mention what had happened to her mother, *never*. Did she understand that? When her mother came back from her 'holiday' Melody had to be quiet and helpful and no bother or else her mother might go away and never come back.

It probably hadn't been the woman's intention, Melody thought, but she'd made the little girl she'd been then feel responsible for everything bad that had happened. For the hours of crying her mother had done in the weeks and months leading up to the attempted suicide, for the way her mother had cuddled her desperately one minute and then flung her aside to indulge in more moaning and crying the next.

'They said it was a breakdown,' Anna said now. 'All I know is I went to hell and back and took you with me for most of it.'

'You were so changed when you came back,' Melody murmured. 'You didn't hold me or kiss me; you rarely even touched me.'

'I didn't dare. Inside I wanted to but I was scared I

might start giving way again. I had to be in control at all times and that meant not letting anything stir me. If I didn't let myself feel I could get by—just. Then I started the business and it became both a blessing and a curse, giving us what we needed materially but sucking me dry of time and energy and life. And understandably I'd lost you by then; you were such a reserved, polite little thing, with great, sad eyes and a way of coping I could only admire. You didn't need me because I'd made you not need me.'

'I did, oh, I did. I do.' Melody's voice was fierce. She hadn't realised it but the inbuilt warning system that she mustn't upset her mother in any way, the dark cloud that descended when she thought of her childhood, the cautionary voice in her head that had always told her she had to be emotionally self-sufficient and not rely on any one person all came from this one incident she'd buried in her mind. It had shaped her more dramatically than her father leaving or her mother's bitterness and withdrawal in the following years. Terrified her so much the only way she'd been able to cope was to put it in a box in her mind and throw away the key.

The two of them talked for the rest of the afternoon and late into the evening, sharing a meal before Melody left. She arrived home absolutely drained, almost too tired to put one foot in front of the other.

Her phone was flashing when she let herself into the bedsit and when she played the answering machine back Zeke's deep voice filled the room. 'Hi.' His voice was smoky, lazy, and her nerves tingled. 'Just to let you know your mother and I survived our encounter without too many scratches and bruises. This week's going to be crazy but I wondered if you're free at the weekend? I'm up in Scotland from Tuesday but I should be back late Friday.

Give me a call and let me know what you think.' There was the slightest of pauses, and then he said very softly, 'Bye, sweetheart.'

She didn't know why but the way he had said 'sweetheart' brought such a poignant twist to her heart it took five minutes before she felt composed enough to ring him back.

He answered immediately in his usual cryptic fashion. 'Zeke Russell.'

'It's me.'

'Hi, me.' The tone had changed, the warm smokiness she'd detected earlier coming through.

'Hi.' She found she was a little breathless. 'I'm sorry I was out earlier; I popped round to see my mother.'

'Checking on war wounds?' he said with dark amusement.

'Something like that.' She took a deep breath. 'Zeke, she said you were great. Thanks. We…we had a good chat.'

Something in her voice must have alerted him to the fact that there was more to that statement than met the eye. 'Are you OK?' he said softly.

Not really. If she was being truthful she'd have to say she didn't know if she was on foot or horseback after all that had happened in the last forty-eight hours. 'I'm fine.'

'Melody, remember we said we were going to talk this time round?' he said evenly. 'So I'll try again. Are you OK?'

She hesitated. She felt emotionally raw and more exposed than she'd ever done. She tried to say something but the lump in her throat was choking her and all that emerged was a low moan.

'I'm coming over.'

'No.' She managed to speak through the tears. 'There's no need. I'm—'

But the phone had gone dead. She stared at the receiver in her hand for some moments before slowly replacing it. She ought to change into something slinkier than the old, well-washed jeans and little top she was wearing before he arrived; brush her hair and renew her mascara and lip gloss. The thought was there but she made no effort to obey it or even to wipe the tears away.

Eventually she walked over and switched on the coffee-machine before finding a box of tissues and blowing her nose hard. Control. She had to get control. This was absolutely ridiculous. He already thought she was a headcase and she was doing nothing to change his opinion.

By the time Zeke rang the bell she'd washed her face and combed her hair through but that was all. She met him on the landing. 'You needn't have come,' she said quickly as he reached her. 'You've got a hectic week in front of you.'

'You're the only thing in front of me right now.' He took her face in his big hands. 'What gives?'

'Come inside.' The last thing they needed was Caroline poking her head out of her door. Once inside the room she closed the door, resolutely refusing to fling herself into his arms, however tempting it was. She had to show him she wasn't falling to pieces. 'It's nothing to do with us,' she said quickly as the amber eyes pierced her face. 'Just something that happened a long time ago. I'd forgotten but when I was talking with my mother something triggered the memory. Do you want a coffee?' she added belatedly.

'Damn the coffee.' He drew her over to the sofa and sat down, pulling her onto his lap. 'Tell me.'

So she did. She kept herself very straight and stiff on his lap because it was the only way she could get through the telling, and when she finally stopped he said nothing, simply folding her into his chest and holding her very close for a long time. She was too spent to do more than relax against him.

Eventually he said, 'I'd give the world for five minutes alone with your father.'

It wasn't what she'd expected. She stirred, sitting up so she could see his face. 'He could be dead for all I know,' she said, shocked by the raw fury in the narrowed eyes. 'And anyway, it doesn't matter now. It was all such a long time ago.'

'It matters because he's still hurting you,' Zeke said in a tone that belied the glittering eyes.

'He's not.' She was surprised and it showed. 'I can barely remember him, to be honest.' It was the shouting and screaming in the days before her father had walked out on them she remembered, not him as a man, as a person.

'Then the results of what he did to your mother are still hurting you—her attempted suicide and how she is now.'

She couldn't argue with the truth of that.

'True?' he persisted very gently.

Unable to speak, Melody settled for a slight nod of the head.

'She needs help, your mother. Professional help. Someone objective who can untangle all the threads and show her how to deal with each knot before moving on to the next one. Your talk today is the first step but it's not enough. You do realise that, don't you?'

Again she could only nod.

'How do you think she'd take to a suggestion she sees someone?'

Melody smiled wanly. 'Like a bull to a red flag.'

'They say bulls only see black and white; it's the fluttering of the flag they object to. She might surprise you.'

Fluttering flags or no fluttering flags, Melody doubted

it. However, she could see the wisdom in Zeke's words. The longer she'd talked with her mother that afternoon, the more she had understood just how mixed-up and unhappy Anna was. The betrayal and desperation her mother had experienced all those years before which had led to the attempted suicide was the bitter root from which many more emotional problems had grown.

'I'll have a word with her.' And then, because the thought which had nagged at her since the night before wouldn't be denied, she added, 'I'm surprised you haven't suggested I see a shrink too.'

'I wouldn't dare.'

His breath tickled her ear and, although she wanted to remain completely lucid and follow up on his reply, her senses were swimming at the smell and feel of him. She struggled to pull herself together. She needed to know what he really thought about her but he was a master of controlling a conversation to his advantage. Parry and thrust were second nature to him. 'I mean it, Zeke,' she began. 'You must be thinking—'

'That you're edible,' he finished for her, turning her into him with a deftness that spoke of experience. She tried to pull away as his lips met hers—she *really* did want to know if he thought she was nuts—but his hands held her face, persuading her to meet his kiss. It was an intoxicating kiss, long and warm, without reserve. She couldn't fight the thrillingly intimate skill she remembered had been so powerful in the past, and almost immediately she felt herself begin to respond.

His lips left hers for a moment, moving over her cheek to her ear, then her temple, then the tip of her small nose before returning to her half-open mouth. She felt herself drowning in the taste of him, his warmth and scent, the hard feel of his shoulders as she clung to him and the lean male thighs beneath her.

She could feel the steady thud-thud of his heart beneath the solid muscles of his broad chest, and the way his heartbeat had quickened would have told her he was aroused, even if another part of his anatomy hadn't borne ample evidence of his desire. She wriggled slightly, teasing him, and he groaned.

His mouth deepened the kiss with deliberate slowness, tantalising her senses and punishing her for the teasing until the pleasure running through her body made her forget everything but him. How could she have done without him for six months? she asked herself dreamily. *How would she do without him in the future if it didn't work out between them?* He had been careful to make no promises this time round.

It was enough to bring her out of the whirling vortex and back into the real world. 'Coffee,' she said shakily. 'I'll fix us both a cup, shall I?'

'Good idea.' It was very dry.

By the time Melody had poured the dark, fragrant liquid into two mugs she'd recovered her composure. Zeke was sitting on the sofa, one leg crossed across the other knee and his arms stretching out along the low back. His natural physical presence and easy sexuality was heightened, rather than lessened, by the casual pose.

She silently berated herself for her racing heart and wondered why everything about him attracted her so intensely. Physically he was almost aggressively masculine, the incredible width of his shoulders and the hard, lean look to his body uncompromising. But there were lots of good-looking men in the world. Zeke had something more.

She fetched out a tin of chocolate digestives and added it to the coffee tray.

He had a magnetic quality, something that whispered of authority and power and pure maleness, and she knew she wasn't the only woman to be drawn by its silent appeal. He only had to look at her for her skin to tingle. It had always been that way.

So why her? She carried the tray over to the sofa, aware of the amber gaze fixed on her face. Why should he want her above the other women, who made it only too plain they were willing and available? She found it unbelievable if she stopped to think about it, which had always been a problem from day one. But she had to believe it. If there was any chance of a tomorrow for them. He had made that plain the night before. It came under the heading of trusting him and she couldn't duck this one.

'You're tuckered,' he said very softly as she sat down beside him.

Occasionally his American origins were obvious and when this happened she became more aware of the slight burr to his voice. It was devastatingly sexy.

She raised her head and looked at him, and the golden gaze was dark and intense. She wondered what was going on behind it. 'I am tired,' she agreed quietly, 'but I'm so glad you came tonight. I didn't want to drag you out but it's…nice.'

'Nice?' He smiled and her heart did a little back flip. 'That's such a very English word, like afternoon tea at the Ritz. I'd prefer something a little more…'

'Imaginative?'

'Intimate.' He drank the coffee straight down, scalding hot, and stood to his feet. 'I'll see myself out. You sit and drink your coffee, unless you want me to stay and tuck you up in bed, that is?' he added with a quirk of one eyebrow.

There was nothing she'd like more. She managed what

she considered was a fairly nonchalant smile as she rose, her coffee untouched. 'Goodnight, Zeke,' she said softly, needing him to kiss her again.

He obliged.

CHAPTER SEVEN

AFTER all the turbulent emotion of the weekend, the next five days were a definite anticlimax.

Zeke phoned before he left for Scotland and arranged that he would come and pick her up on Saturday morning. 'A colleague of mine has offered his boat at Henley-on-Thames for the day,' he said lazily. 'Might be…nice. What do you think?'

She grinned into the phone. 'Very…nice.'

'Good.' There was a pause, and then he added, 'This is a business trip to Scotland, Melody. You understand what that entails?' All amusement had gone from his voice.

She hadn't. Not till that moment. 'Your secretary is accompanying you.' She couldn't bring herself to say Angela's name, even though she knew there was nothing between them beyond a working relationship. But the other woman was still going to be with him for four whole days…and nights.

'Right,' he said flatly.

She braced herself. 'That's fine,' she said breezily. 'Why shouldn't it be?'

There was a pause and when he spoke again he hadn't answered her question, merely arranging a time to call on

Saturday morning. Melody had put down the phone feeling acutely disturbed. She'd got the feeling he had read her mind with no difficulty at all.

She had a word with her mother the next evening. 'No!' Anna shook her head in rapid movement, her cheeks flushing scarlet. 'How could you even suggest such a thing? I'm not crazy.'

'I never said you were and I'm talking a counsellor here, not a psychiatrist,' Melody said patiently.

'In this instance it's the same thing and you know it.'

'No, it is not, and no, I don't. You suffered a very real bereavement when Dad left, worse than if he'd died. You never talked it through with anyone at the time; you told me yourself they didn't even offer that sort of help at the hospital after…'

The look on her mother's face stopped her from continuing. Melody sighed. 'Look, just think about it, will you?' she asked, standing up preparatory to leaving. She'd had dinner with her mother and had thought it best to bring up the subject of Anna seeing someone just as she left. That way she could leave before the main fallout and her mother might start mulling everything over in her mind.

'I don't have to.'

'I'm only saying this because I love you.' Melody was determined they weren't going to slip back into the old ways and now she took her mother into her arms, hugging her tight and kissing her.

There was a moment when she thought Anna wasn't going to respond and then her mother hugged her back, holding on to her very tight for a moment or two.

'And don't worry about the business, OK?' Melody added as they stood on the doorstep in the damp warmth of a rainy May evening. 'Everything will work out.' Her

mother had told her that whatever Zeke had said to Julian
had worked because the other man had done the grand con-
fession by way of a letter to the opposing firm's solicitors.
They had yet to see if the firm were appeased at all or
whether their action would be deflected away from Anna.
Julian was pleading a mental breakdown for his actions and
it seemed his doctor was prepared to go along with it.

She was getting ready for work the next morning when
her mother rang her. 'Do you know any good counsellors
through your work?' Anna asked abruptly without even
saying hello or good morning. 'And it would have to be a
woman; I couldn't cope with talking to a man about everything.'

Melody tried to keep her voice bland and matter-of-fact.
'A couple, as it happens. Do you want me to have a word
and see if either of them is free in the next day or two for
an initial private consultation?' Having got her mother this
far she didn't want her to have too much time to sit and
think and change her mind.

By eleven o'clock that morning she'd arranged for Anna
to see a charming middle-aged lady whose small surgery
was only a stone's throw from her mother's front door. It
seemed a good omen somehow.

A couple of panics at work during the end of the week
had Melody worrying she wouldn't be able to see Zeke on
Saturday, but then, miraculously, everything cleared within
hours on Friday afternoon although it meant she was very
late home. She found she was ridiculously excited and
nervous at the same time and couldn't eat any of the light
cold-meat salad she prepared for her supper.

A long, leisurely bath relaxed her to some extent but she
was still a bundle of nerves when the phone rang just after
ten o'clock. She turned off the news—which was a cata-

logue of murder, mayhem and natural disasters and was as depressing as always—and padded across in bare feet to answer it.

'I'm just about to step on a plane to bring me home but I wanted to catch you before you went to bed.' Zeke's voice was warm and soft. 'To tell you to dream of me. OK?'

Did he seriously think she ever did anything else?

'And to say I've missed you.'

Missed you. Not that he loved her but that he'd missed her, but then, after how she'd behaved, missing was more than she had any right to expect. 'Ditto,' she managed, a little breathlessly.

'What are you wearing right now? I want to picture you in my mind,' he said huskily.

It gave her enormous satisfaction when—after telling the truth and saying she was naked under her bathrobe—she heard him groan. 'That's not fair,' he said plaintively. 'Couldn't you have lied and told me you were togged up to your ears?'

'I never lie,' she said primly. 'I'm a good girl.'

'I'm going to have to work on that.'

Yes, please. 'How was the trip?' she asked carefully. 'Satisfactory?'

'Overall. It's to do with a complicated case, though; an unpleasant one.'

Melody nodded although he couldn't see her. 'It never fails to amaze me the depths some human beings can sink to.'

'You're lucky,' he said drily. 'I lost the ability to be amazed years ago. Comes with the territory, I guess.'

She heard a woman's voice in the background and then he said, 'I have to go. We're boarding. See you tomorrow, sweetheart.'

Another 'sweetheart'. Her heart was singing when she put down the phone in spite of the fact it had undoubtedly been Angela she'd heard. He had used to call her sweetheart before, so that was a good sign, wasn't it?

He had also used to call her every night without fail wherever he was six months ago, a nasty little voice in the back of her mind reminded her, and this was the first time she had heard from him since Monday night. She'd been struggling with the thought all week. She frowned. OK, the damage she'd done couldn't be mended in a moment but they were seeing each other again and that was all that mattered. Nevertheless she didn't sleep well that night.

At six o'clock the next morning she was wide awake and watching the sun rise in a cloudless blue sky, a blue as hard and still as a painting. It was going to be a beautiful day—the first day of June. She hoped the good weather would hold until next Saturday when Brad and Kate got married.

Brushing the thought of the wedding aside, she made herself a coffee and drank it back in bed, her stomach doing the occasional cartwheel at the thought of a whole day and evening with Zeke. She didn't know why she was so jittery, or then again, maybe she did. She didn't want anything to spoil things this second time round but it still seemed too good to be true that they were back together, and when things seemed too good to be true it was usually because they were.

She shut her eyes tight for a moment and then opened them wide. All week she'd been plagued with darts of doubt about him in one way or another. It seemed the years of programming by her mother couldn't be shaken off in just a few days, however hard she tried. And she had been trying.

She was ready and waiting long before the buzzer on the front door sounded just before nine. She had met Caroline on the landing at half-past seven when leaving the bathroom—the other girl had just got in from a night on the tiles with a group of friends, but although she'd drunk and danced the night away she looked as fresh as a daisy.

On learning Melody was going out with Zeke for the day Caroline had raised her eyebrows and pursed her lips before saying, 'It's still all on, then? Keeping him hungry like I told you?'

'It's not like that with Zeke and me.'

'It's *always* like that when a man is drop-dead gorgeous. You have to be one step ahead of the competition until you've snared his heart as well as his—' Caroline pointed downwards. 'Now, what are you wearing for a smoochy day on the river? Has this boat got a cabin and a double bed?'

'I've no idea,' said Melody, laughing. 'I was going to wear jeans and a top for practicality—you know, getting on and off the boat and so on.'

Caroline screeched her horror. 'Forget practical, for crying out loud! You want to wow him, don't you? You've got gorgeous legs—show 'em off. It's going to be a lovely hot day; you can get away with as little as possible.'

Melody looked at the minute mini-skirt and glittering vest-top Caroline was wearing—neither left anything to the imagination. 'I don't think so,' she began doubtfully.

'Come on.' Caroline pulled her along the corridor. 'Show me your wardrobe and I'll pick out something that will be sure to set his juices flowing.'

A few minutes later she was smiling in satisfaction. 'Perfect,' she said, draping the white sun-dress over the back of one of the dining chairs. 'Shame it's white and not a sexy red or something, but that low front and non-existent back is dynamite, along with all those slits in the skirt. It looks like an ordinary full skirt until you move and then—' she rolled wicked eyes '—very naughty. I haven't seen you in that before, have I?'

Melody shook her head, her hair still damp from the bath. 'I haven't worn it before,' she admitted weakly.

She had actually bought the sun-dress at the end of November, shortly after she'd split up with Zeke. It had featured in the window of an expensive designer shop she passed every morning on her way to work, and the end-of-season sale had been stunningly good.

She hadn't realised about the thigh-length splits in the calf-length skirt until she had tried the dress on, at which point she had decided she'd never have the nerve to wear it. With the low-cut broderie-anglaise bodice and non-existent back to the dress, the few scraps of material holding the whole thing together had suddenly seemed too fragile, if not indecent.

But the shop assistant had enthused and it had fitted her perfectly, the dramatic reduction in cost persuading her it was probably simpler to buy it just in case she ever had a chance to wear anything so different to her usual modest taste. That and the fact that Zeke's supposed affair with the sensuous, provocative Angela was still blindingly raw, and she just knew the other woman wouldn't think twice about wearing what was an undeniably beautiful—but innocently wanton—dress.

Melody fingered the folds in the skirt. 'I don't know,' she said doubtfully.

'Melody, it's stunning. Trust me.' Caroline sighed at the look on her friend's face. 'Look, there's not a breath of wind out there today, no breeze, nothing. The skirt's not going to blow in the slightest and when you walk there's only a glimpse of leg.' She glanced at the other dresses she'd made Melody try on, wrinkling her freckled nose as she said, 'Those are just too ordinary in comparison. You *have* to wear this. Don't you want to make him realise you could have any man you want? Make him just a teeny weeny bit jealous?'

She thought Caroline was overdoing it on the any-man-she-wanted bit but the dress *was* gorgeous and perfect for a baking hot day as this one promised to be. And he had been in the company of the voluptuous Angela all week. Absolutely innocent, totally business, but still…

She had been waiting in the lobby of the house for a good few minutes when she saw the shadow of his shape through the frosted glass in the front door a moment before he pressed the buzzer. She hadn't been able to face the thought of sashaying down the stairs in front of him. She slipped on the little short-sleeved light-blue cotton cardigan which matched the blue pumps on her feet before she opened the door. She didn't feel quite so naked with her back covered.

'Hi there,' he said very softly as she stood framed in the doorway, his tawny eyes narrowed against the glare of the white sunlight outside. He was dressed in light trousers and a pale grey shirt, the sleeves rolled up and the collar open at the neck. He looked as sexy as sin and twice as dangerous.

For a moment Melody forgot to breathe. 'Hi.'

'Come here.'

The excuse she'd had for hovering in the lobby like a lovesick teenager wasn't needed because in the next second he'd taken her in his arms, kissing her very thoroughly before he let her go long enough to say, 'Missed me?'

He'd never know how much. A little tremor at his power

over her raced all through her, but she managed to keep her expression bright when she said teasingly, 'Now and again.'

'Only now and again? I must be losing my touch. I'll have to try harder.' He took her hand, lowering his head and sliding his warm lips against her curved palm before tracing a tingling path over her wrist, where his mouth hovered over her frantic pulse.

His dark hair shone with clean health, the faint, delicious smell of his aftershave mingling with primitive male scent, and Melody had to bite her lower lip hard not to give in to the desire to moan out loud. He was barely touching her, not really, and yet he could reduce her to a quivering wreck with such little effort. And he knew it.

As Zeke raised smiling narrowed eyes Melody looked into their sparkling amber depths and she knew he was aware of exactly how he affected her. She blinked. She didn't like that but she was at a loss to know how to change it.

Her head rose very slightly and she extricated her hand, smiling as though she hadn't a care in the world. 'Shall we go?' she said evenly. 'It's a beautiful day, isn't it?'

'Very beautiful,' he said softly, but he was looking at her.

Damn that dress she was wearing. As Zeke watched Melody slide into the car before he closed the door his body went haywire. He had enough trouble controlling himself at the best of times but today... She'd looked so demure, standing there in virginal white with her little blue shoes—although the soft swell of her breasts revealed in the low bodice had sent the blood surging—and then she had walked to the car.

There were times when he had to avoid even the most elementary of contact, knowing instinctively that one touch, one kiss and he wouldn't be able to stop. And he didn't want it to be like that with Melody. He hadn't wanted it in the past when he'd thought she was going to be his wife and he didn't want it now—however this turned out. Because she didn't want it, not at the heart of her. Oh, he knew he could make love to her and she wouldn't stop him—wouldn't *want* to stop him. It would be mind-blowing for both of them. But it would spoil something for her, take away the dream, and she'd had enough dreams spoilt in her life.

They were light-years apart in so many ways and yet when they had been together he'd felt she was his other half, the completion of him, and that without full intimacy. He had actually trembled when he'd imagined their wedding night. His mouth twisted in wry self-deprecation when he thought of how friends and ex-girlfriends would have reacted to such knowledge.

At twelve he'd discovered the opposite sex and at fifteen he'd been initiated into the pleasures of the flesh by an experienced eighteen-year-old. There had followed some wild years which had encompassed his time at university, but with law school had come hard work and discipline and one steady relationship at a time. But he had never remotely wanted to settle down. In fact, in spite of his parents' happy marriage, he hadn't been sure if he believed in the concept of monogamy until he had met Melody.

He opened the driver's door, mentally preparing himself for the scented warmth of her as he slid into his seat. It didn't help the physical reaction one iota. There were times he felt his body was being dipped in hot oil by the strength of his desire. When he'd asked her to marry him and told her it would have to be a short engagement it was because he needed to protect his sanity!

'What?' She was looking at him, her eyes enquiring.

'I didn't say anything.' He started the engine and pulled out into the morning traffic.

'I know, but you were smiling…sort of.'

'How do you 'sort of' smile?'

'When you don't really like what you're smiling at, when it's not funny.'

Ain't that the truth! Zeke forced himself to relax tense muscles, his face impassive and his voice mild when he said, 'I'll put any unfunny thoughts on the back burner for the rest of the day. How's that?'

Out of the corner of his eye he saw her glance at him and he knew she was aware of the prevarication by the look on her face. She said nothing, however, merely turning again to look out of the window a moment later.

What was she thinking? All the time he was concentrating on the busy road ahead his mind was dissecting information sent through his senses. He knew he could turn her on physically, that had never been in any doubt in the past and it wasn't now. But he wanted more than a willing partner to warm his bed for the future. His wife, the mother of his children would be different. It had been the biggest shock in his life when she had walked away from him without a backward glance. He'd had no idea anything was wrong and then the next minute she'd exited his life. Because she didn't trust him. Maybe she still didn't.

He knew he had a reputation for ruthlessness and maybe even arrogance in the field in which he worked, and he used it to his advantage when he had to. But with Melody he'd felt that side of him stripped away almost from the first time they had met. It had scared him to death at first, he admitted it, but then he had come to terms with the vulnerability being in love brought in its wake.

He still hadn't liked it. He dodged round a family saloon that seemed to think it was in a 5 mph zone. But he'd accepted it. But he really didn't know if he could survive the cauterising cycle once more if he asked her to marry him for a second time and then she upped and left at some point.

Men were supposed to be strong and stable whatever happened to them, able to face the darkest of situations with a cavalier spirit to carry them through. But when Melody had walked out on him his world had been rocked to its foundations. He hadn't cried. He had felt as if he was out of his body, numb, dead for weeks, and when the feeling had gradually seeped back in raw strips of time he'd felt as though he was going insane.

The only source of comfort had been that he knew— through a guy he had come into contact with through the courts and who worked for a detective agency—that Melody wasn't involved with someone else. He hadn't attempted to work out what he would do if that changed.

All he knew now was that he'd have no one to blame if this went sour the second time round. He'd walked into it with his eyes wide open. Crazy, impossible situation. Crazy, impossible *woman*.

Melody stirred at the side of him and her body heat released her perfume, vanilla, wisteria and musk coupled with her own personal scent bringing a sensual fragrance to Zeke's nostrils. He forced himself to concentrate on the road ahead; London traffic didn't allow for dips into suffocatingly erotic fantasies, he thought wryly as he slammed the door shut on his frustrated libido.

Zeke's friend was waiting for them when they arrived at Henley-on-Thames, and it was clear his boat was his pride and joy as he showed them over the smart little cruiser, pointing out the dual steering and sliding roof with inordinate pride. After chatting for a few minutes he disappeared off to his car, leaving the two of them alone.

It *was* a dear little boat. Melody glanced round the saloon, which was fitted with a TV and video, as well as a stereo system and all mod cons in the neatly fitted-out galley and main rear cabin. A home from home.

She joined Zeke on the raised sundeck, her heart flipping over at the boyish enthusiasm in his handsome face. For a moment he looked years younger and it touched her more than she liked. He had told her stories of his boyhood, of running wild in the vast state in America he'd been born in and all the adventures he and his friends had indulged in, and just for an instant she thought she had caught a glimpse of what he would have looked like then. The cynical, somewhat stern face had mellowed and his eyes were alight with anticipation.

'Do you want to steer or shall I?' he asked with barely concealed eagerness, pulling her close as she went to stand by him.

'I wouldn't dare spoil your fun,' she teased, laughing as he grinned back at her, totally unabashed.

'But first we toast Crystal,' Zeke said, patting the boat fondly as though it were listening before disappearing into the little galley, where he'd placed the big wicker picnic basket he'd brought with him. He soon reappeared with two fluted glasses of sparkling champagne in his hands.

'I thought picnics were supposed to consist of curling cucumber sandwiches and warm lemonade?' Melody took her glass with a nod of thanks.

'Not my sort,' said Zeke very definitely. 'We've got canapés, mini-soufflés, goat's cheese and Parma-ham galettes, spring rolls, prawn wontons, apricot stuffing and bacon wraps, king prawns in a lime cream dip—'

'Stop, stop.' Melody was laughing.

'Don't you want to know what's for dessert?'

'No.' Her eyes were caught by his and the rest of the world suddenly ceased to exist. The warm sun caressing her skin, the feel of the dress swishing about her bare legs, the dark, handsome man looking at her with hungry eyes were intoxicating. 'Surprise me later,' she whispered, unaware of just how much her face was revealing.

'I might do that.' He seemed reluctant to touch her now and Melody knew a dart of something which could have been hurt—if she had analysed it—pierce her as Zeke took a physical step backwards before lifting his glass. 'To Crystal and the day,' he said evenly, his eyes glowing a deep golden colour which was almost iridescent in the sunlight.

'To Crystal and the day,' Melody echoed, even as she thought, Not to us?

The champagne was ice-cold and fruity on her tongue, the bubbles tasting faintly of strawberries. Melody continued to sip hers as Zeke eased the boat away from its mooring and out into the river. There was all manner of craft on the water, a long, brightly coloured narrowboat passing as Zeke waited for the opportunity to slot into the mainstream. Two small children waved excitedly to Melody and she waved back.

An hour later she was lying on a blanket on the sundeck—her dress carefully positioned for maximum suntanning effect whilst still remaining decent—watching Zeke from under cover of her eyelashes. He was steering the boat and apparently engrossed in what he was doing. Melody wriggled restlessly. She moved slightly so the dress fell away from the top of one leg, revealing an inordinate amount of smooth thigh. Zeke didn't notice.

'This is lovely.' She sat up, leaning backwards on her elbows. 'Do you want another glass of champagne?'

'Not for me.' He flashed her an easy smile. 'Only one when I'm driving. I wouldn't say no to some of that sparkling mineral water I've brought, though.'

'Right.' Feeling more than a little piqued at his lack of interest, she rose to her feet and padded barefoot down into the galley, pouring the glass of mineral water before—with a little touch of defiance—she tipped some more champagne into her own flute.

Once on deck again, she handed Zeke his glass, standing next to him as she sipped at her own. The glittering water, the smooth green lawns and beautiful houses they were passing all added to the magic of the day. She breathed deeply of the summer air, shutting her eyes and just relishing the moment.

His lips were cool from the water as they skimmed hers in a fleeting kiss which nevertheless sent her sense spinning out of control for a moment or two. She opened her eyes to see his laughing as he said, 'Couldn't resist that.'

'Feel free,' said Melody, smiling back.

His hand came up to tuck a strand of silky blonde hair behind her ear and his fingers lingered at her throat for a moment, stroking the sun-warmed skin before they feathered across the smooth swell of her cleavage. 'That dress is something else,' he murmured throatily.

'I didn't think you'd noticed.' Her voice was calm and light, she noted with satisfaction.

He grinned. 'I noticed,' he said casually, his tone matching hers.

Her eyes were on his face and the muscle that jumped in his jaw belied his nonchalant voice. Her pulse gave a funny little leap and then raced away like a bolting horse.

He reached down and picked up the glass of water again, taking a long pull before he said evenly, 'Melody, I think I need to make something perfectly clear. You excite me every time I look at you, OK? So just to keep the record straight you don't have to fish for compliments. I want you. I don't deny I meet plenty of women on a day-to-day basis but you are different. I'm not even sure I can put my finger on the reason to explain why but it's been that way since the first time we met. You are beautiful and intelligent and with or without that dress you turn me on to the point of insanity.'

She didn't know what to say. She shook her head help-lessly. 'I want you too,' she managed breathlessly.

'I know.' He glanced straight into her eyes for a second, no arrogance in either his face or his voice. 'But wanting isn't enough, not for me.'

The words were like a dash of cold water on her psyche. She felt a lead weight plummet in her stomach and just stared at the hard-planed profile as he turned back to guiding the boat.

'I want everything or nothing.' He paused. 'That's just the way it is with how I feel about you. And everything includes your commitment and love, but more than that, your trust and faith. In me. As a man.'

His tone was completely neutral now and she realised he was voicing something he had thought about very care-fully.

'I…I do trust you.'

'Do you?' Again the tawny gaze swept piercingly over her face. 'I would like to think so but I've never been one for fooling myself. Perhaps that's why I chose to be a lawyer; I prize the truth above most else.' His lips twisted. 'Once I would have said above everything but meeting you has made me face the fact that if I could accept your words at face value and believe we had a chance, I'd forget the truth. But we *wouldn't* have a chance—not the forever kind anyway. Sooner or later without trust things would fall apart again. Do you understand that?'

She pinched one of the folds in her skirt, unable to look at him any longer. She was terrified. He was telling her it was over. Here, on the river, on the most beautiful day of the summer he was going to exit her life. She swallowed hard. 'What exactly are you saying?'

'That you have to face certain facts over the next little while and not brush them under the carpet,' Zeke said gently. 'For my sake as well as yours. I don't want to drift on as we are now, not for any length of time. I can't,' he added raggedly. 'Our relationship went through its probationary period six months ago and we made the decision to get married. I had fully committed. You hadn't.'

And then, as Melody went to interrupt in protest, he said, 'Think about it. You know it's the truth.'

The silence lengthened between them, a dog barking on the lawn of a stately mansion they were passing and children calling to each other on a nearby boat barely registering on Melody's consciousness.

'I'm greedy, sweetheart.'

As she looked up at the sound of his voice he touched her mouth with the gentlest of kisses. 'Zeke—'

'No.' He stopped her from speaking with a finger on her lips. 'This was not a conversation that required you to make promises or even say anything at all.' A wry smile curved his lips but the golden eyes were purposely without expression as they met hers. 'But I need you to start facing the gremlins and deciding whether you're going to give me all of you. Like I said, I'm greedy. Maybe another man would be content for you to hold back but I'm not built that way. I want you for my wife, Melody. I want to have children with you and grow old with you. I always have. But this isn't a proposal. It's a statement of how I would like things to be if you make it possible. If you learn to trust me.'

She nodded. Slowly, painfully, full comprehension dawned. 'Do you think a person can learn trust?' she whispered. 'Surely it's either there or it isn't.'

Zeke caught his breath for a moment before letting it out in a sigh. 'I've asked myself the same question over the last few days and yes, I think trust and faith in another human being are things which can be learnt if the circumstances are right, if the *people* are right, however damaged or disillusioned one or both of them are.'

'But you aren't damaged or disillusioned.'

One eyebrow rose laconically.

'But you think I am,' she said, knowing he was right but not wanting to admit it out loud with the sunshine and the brightness of the day mocking the seriousness of the conversation.

He still didn't say anything. As Melody studied him, she felt another kind of fear surface—the fear that she wouldn't be able to be what she needed to be for their relationship to survive.

He was being overwhelmingly reasonable in the circumstances. Her eyes drifted over the big masculine body as he concentrated on the river ahead and oncoming boats, her attention caught by the way his trousers fitted over a very firm, trim rear end. The width of his shoulders, the way his coal-black hair just touched the collar of his shirt, his large, capable hands on the wheel of the boat—he was gorgeous, she told herself miserably. Absolutely gorgeous. And she couldn't live without him. But he had made it plain he could and would live without her if he had to.

She braced her hip against the side of the boat and looked out over the water to the bank, trying to derive a sense of calm from the normality of the scene in front of her. It was understandable that he feared being hurt all over again, understandable that he felt she was something of a loose cannon. How could she convince him otherwise? *Did* she wholly and unreservedly trust him? Her body was so tense it hurt and she finished the champagne in one gulp. She didn't want to delve too deep into that one but he'd made it clear she had to.

Her head turned again and she took in the strong planes of his jaw, the determined thrust to his chin. She loved his chin; she'd always delighted in stroking her tongue over the little cleft in it.

She wasn't sure how long she stood there, lost in myriad thoughts, her mind travelling from one problem, one incident, one memory to another and then another. Suddenly she realised they'd pulled into a little backwater shaded from the noonday sun by overhanging branches of leafy trees. The sunlight was dappled now, the air cooler and scented with the wild flowers starring the edge of the riverbank.

She felt rather than saw Zeke lean towards her, his voice soft as he said, 'Stop worrying, just enjoy the day.' His hand caught hers and he pulled her gently into his arms. She stood very still as he began to stroke her hair without saying anything more and gradually she began to relax against him, to float on a delicious, dreamy cloud of warmth and sensuality. When his fingers tightened at the back of her head, tilting her face upwards as his lips took hers, she was more than ready for the kiss.

It was a soft kiss, a slow kiss, and a heady tingling began deep within her body, spreading along nerves and sinews until she felt she was melting. He had always been so good at kissing, she told herself almost resentfully. She had never met any man who could kiss like Zeke.

Let go of the fear. Stop letting it spoil your life. The message from her brain straight into the core of her emotions was so sudden it was almost as if someone had spoken it. Shaken, she instinctively tightened her hold on Zeke and at the same moment he lifted his head, his hands moving to her waist. 'How about some lunch?' he said easily, drawing her with him towards the galley before she had a chance to answer. 'I don't know about you but I'm starving.'

What she was starving for wouldn't be assuaged by canapés and Parma-ham galettes, however delicious they might be, Melody thought ruefully. But she couldn't very well say so.

They ate at the little table in the galley and because Zeke put himself out to be amusing the meal was one of laughter and warmth. For dessert Zeke magicked two rich and decadent chocolate rum tortes from the boat's little fridge. Made with Belgian chocolate and ground hazelnuts and topped with dark flakes of chocolate and rum ganache, they stood in round terracotta pots and tasted heavenly.

'I'm so full I could burst.' As they lingered over coffee, Melody reached out her hand and grasped Zeke's. 'Thank you for such a wonderful meal and a wonderful day.'

'It isn't finished yet.'

'I know.' She smiled at him and he smiled back.

'And now a nap, I think.' He drained his coffee-cup and

stood up, pulling her with him. 'How about we stretch out on the sundeck for an hour and take in some rays?'

She nodded. It had been a hectic week for her and she knew it had for him; the big meal and the warmth of the day had made her sleepy.

Zeke spread out the blanket she had lain on earlier, taking off his shoes and socks and then his shirt. Melody stood watching him, suddenly feeling like a fourteen-year-old schoolgirl at the sight of his muscled bare chest. Ridiculous, she told herself, but somehow it was more intimate than if he had no clothes on at all.

He had lain down on the blanket before he became aware of her standing still. 'Come on.' He lifted a lazy arm. 'Come and get comfy.'

She really didn't think getting comfy was an option, not with that hard male body registering on her senses like fire. But she couldn't stand staring at him all afternoon. She had long since discarded her cardigan and pumps, and now she carefully knelt down and then moved to lie beside him, his arm going round her so that her face ended up buried against his chest. She loved the feel of his rough body hair against her cheek. She loved *everything* about him. She sighed softly.

'You feel good,' he said huskily, his breath tickling her ear.

So do you. Oh, so do you. 'Likewise,' said Melody, pleased with how calm her voice sounded, considering she was going into meltdown.

'I've missed times like this, of being close like this. Just holding you.'

'So have I.' She couldn't help herself; she pressed her lips to the hair-roughened chest. She felt his whole body tighten and knew she was being unfair but perversely she didn't care. Her mouth found the round, hard nub of one nipple.

His voice was strangled when he said, 'Go to sleep, Melody.'

'I don't want to sleep.'

'I do.'

'Oh.' From her vantage point against his chest she could see his body was telling a different story. She moved very slightly, sliding her leg along his, and he groaned softly. 'Zeke—'

'I mean it, Melody. You either go to sleep or I start the boat and we go out on the river again.'

She knew he meant it. She pouted, and then with a quiet exhalation turned to look at him for a moment. 'I love you,' she whispered. It was the first time she had said it since they had got back together again.

He looked back at her for several long seconds, and then there was a tinge of sadness in his voice when he said, 'I love you too. I never stopped loving you.'

It should have made her wildly happy, especially because his eyes were unmasked and vulnerable, his expression as open as in the old days. But it didn't. Because now there was a wariness there too, a reserve that darkened the gold and tinged it with shadow. He was letting her see that loving wasn't enough and it hurt more than his words earlier in the day had done.

'Go to sleep, Melody,' he said again, and this time she lay quiet and still against him, making no movement whatsoever.

It must have been some ten to fifteen minutes before the change in his body and the sound of his even, deep breathing told her he slept. Although her eyelids were heavy and her limbs tired, her mind was too active to follow him.

She moved very carefully so as not to wake him, turning so she lay looking up into the leafy green canopy overhead through which shafts of sunlight streamed. It was deliciously warm in the shady hideaway but without the fierce burning property the sun had held earlier. The swish-swish of the water against the boat, the twittering of birds in the trees overhead and the muted sounds of life from the river beyond all combined to produce a somnolent state which Melody was happy to drift into. She didn't want to think or reason any more, she told herself as her mind slowed down and the soporific mood deepened. She just wanted to be.

When Zeke awoke it was instant, a wide-awake alertness that was habitual, banishing the merest remnant of sleep. From a child he had been that way, much to his mother's disgruntlement. He had never been able to understand the desire of wanting to lie in in the mornings or the need to wake up slowly, and certainly the idea of breakfast in bed or even of reading the Sunday papers in bed was alien to him. Or it had been before he had fallen in love with Melody.

He turned his head and looked at her lying in an abandonment which told him she was fast asleep.

Once he had met her he'd known he would want to do all sorts of things with her he hadn't with the other women he had known. He'd found the sexual act pleasurable with them and one or two had remained good friends when the affair had ended, but the idea of lingering intimacy hadn't been on the cards. He hadn't wanted to wake up with a woman, to have her run his bath or canoodle over breakfast; he hadn't wanted a woman as a *necessary* part of his life. They had fitted into one section of his existence and he had enjoyed them—as he'd hoped they'd enjoyed him. No strings attached, no serious emotional involvement, no stepping into each other's lives beyond the sector in which they functioned. And he would have continued quite happily that way if he hadn't glanced across the court one day and been arrested by a pair of grey eyes set in a face that was truly heart-shaped.

The dress had fallen away from her legs as she slept, the soft swell of her breasts and the silky, slender length of smooth skin causing his loins to tighten and his manhood to swell. He would never be able to get enough of her. If he had her several times a day for the rest of his life it wouldn't be enough to satisfy the hunger inside him. He wanted to fill her, to possess her so completely there was no one and nothing but him in the whole world for her.

A family home, children, a wife who would have the right to expect certain lifelong promises from him—love, faithfulness, responsibility, devotion—had all been concepts he'd have run a hundred miles from before he had met her. He had looked on in pity when one or other of his friends had got himself ensnared by the matrimony trap, going to their weddings and saying all the right things but inwardly congratulating himself that he knew what was what. And it didn't include throwing his freedom away. His liberty. His *existence*.

But that had been then and this was now. *Damn it*. He caught quickly at the anger but not quickly enough, frustration making it difficult to control. He had been so angry with her in the early days after they had broken up, a raw rage eating him day and night once he had allowed himself to start feeling again. It had been a little while before he had realised it wasn't Melody he was mad at so much as her mother, her father, her mockery of a childhood—all the things which had made her into the person she was now, a person who couldn't trust or believe in the opposite sex. And he didn't know half of it, he was certain of that. He had told her all there was about him but she'd been selective.

He sat up carefully so as not to wake Melody, running his fingers through his hair and massaging his temples as he did so. She said she loved him but how much he wasn't sure. The only thing he *was* sure about right now was that he was letting his need outweigh his common sense. His need to be able to see her, touch her, smell her scent and warmth. It didn't sit well with the cold, logical side of him that made him such a damn good lawyer. He smiled grimly.

When the scream rang out from the river beyond their little backwater it hadn't finished before Zeke was on his feet. As he leapt off the boat onto the grass he thought he heard Melody call his name. He didn't stop to look back—the scream had been too spine-chilling—running into the blazing sunlight of the bank bordering the main river in seconds.

It was virtually empty but for boats in the distance and the small craft in the centre of the river. This contained a young woman—still screaming—with a toddler in her arms, another child splashing about in the water before seeming to sink like a stone.

Zeke's dive took him close to the spot where the child had been, and as he became aware of the propeller churning the water—and silently cursed the woman for not cutting the engine—he thought he saw a movement below him but the murky water made it impossible to be sure.

With the blades of the revolving shaft murderously close he kicked with his legs, his hands reaching out in front of him as he clawed through the water for the child...

CHAPTER EIGHT

MELODY stood on the edge of the riverbank with shock billowing through her body. She had arrived moments after Zeke but too late to see where he had dived. All she could do was to shout for the now hysterical mother to turn off the engine. The water that had seemed so attractive earlier was now a thing of horror as her eyes searched its depths, and she wrapped her arms round her waist as the woman on the boat sobbed that her little boy had fallen overboard.

How deep was the river here? She had no idea. And there were weeds in rivers, weren't there? Weeds that wrapped themselves like tentacles round unsuspecting legs and held them fast. Why hadn't she ever learnt to swim? Zeke, oh, Zeke. Why hadn't he surfaced? It must be thirty seconds, even a minute since he'd gone in.

When Zeke materialised, the child clutched in one arm, she thought she was going to faint. Only the fact that he needed her prevented it. The young mother had completely gone to pieces and was no good at all; she had sunk to her knees and seemed unable to let go of the toddler in her arms. Zeke must have realised this because he swam to the bank, choking water as he gasped, 'Take him...he's not breathing.'

'Oh, Zeke.' In her haste she nearly fell in herself, just managing to rebalance herself as she hauled the horribly still body of the child onto the warm grass.

Zeke followed a second later, immediately applying mouth-to-mouth to the tiny, limp scrap. The length of time before the little boy responded, vomiting river water as he began to whimper, was an eternity. Zeke glanced up at her as he sat the child in his lap and began to rub life into the cold little body. 'Phone for an ambulance; he's swallowed a lot of filthy water. Tell them we've just passed a pub called the Crosskeys and we'll meet them there. And bring a blanket back with you.'

He turned from her to the young mother, who was still hysterical, calling out to an approaching boat holding two young couples, 'There's been an accident. See to the mother, would you? Get her over here if you can.'

When Melody arrived back with the blanket after phoning for an ambulance, the other boat had just delivered the mother to her now screaming infant, one of the men steering the woman's boat into the side. With the two couples taking care of the boats, Zeke and Melody—holding a child each and trying to support the mother, who seemed on the verge of collapse—made their way along the bank to the Crosskeys, the ambulance arriving a minute or two after them.

They caused quite a stir at the pub. It wasn't every day a half-naked man covered in slime and dirt carrying an equally bedraggled child arrived, complete with two women in tow and another infant. Especially when—as the landlady was heard to remark to one of her regular women customers later in the day—the man in question had a body to die for.

The ambulancemen tried to persuade Zeke to accompany the young family to the hospital, where a doctor could check him over, but he was having none of it. 'No way,' he said firmly, one arm round Melody, who was clutching him as though *she* was drowning. 'I'm fine.'

But he might not have been. Melody was trying very hard to keep a lid on her emotion but it was hard. She had suddenly been faced with the transient reality of life and it was scary. More than scary—terrifying.

Once Zeke had given his name and address and a quick summary of events, the ambulance sped off, and—refusing the drinks on the house the landlady of the Crosskeys tried to press on them—Zeke and Melody walked back along the riverbank. They walked in silence at first, their hands linked, the enormity of what might have happened to the little boy if they hadn't chosen to moor their boat in the backwater sobering.

'I…I might have lost you,' Melody whispered as they reached the boat, and in spite of the hot day she was shivering. 'I didn't think you were ever going to come up out of that water.'

Zeke grinned. 'It'd take more than a drop or two of water to keep me from you.' And then, seeing the look in her eyes, he pulled her into him, his voice rueful as he said, 'This has been one hell of a relaxing day out for you, hasn't it? It's not quite what I had planned.'

'I'm just glad you're safe—and the little boy. His mother must be one of the dopiest women alive. Fancy taking off their life-jackets so they could have a nap.' Melody shook her head in disbelief. She'd hardly been able to credit it when the woman had given a garbled version of the events leading up to the accident, adding that the twins—apparently the siblings were twins and four years old, and, by the mother's own admission, a handful—had woken up and slipped past her while she was preparing lunch. Their father was working on an oilrig and so out of the immediate picture.

'Look, I'm going to check those couples can stay with the boat until the representative from the boatyard she was going to ring get here, OK? Perhaps you'd see if the shower's working? I need to sluice some of this muck off.'

For a crazy moment Melody almost said that she wanted to go with him, that she couldn't bear to let him out of her sight for a second, but she managed to bite back the impulse. She was a grown woman who held down a very responsible job, she told herself sternly as Zeke walked on and she climbed onto the boat. She couldn't go to pieces. After all, everything had ended well and no harm—hopefully—had come to the little boy in the long run. But when she had gazed at that water for what had seemed a lifetime… She shuddered.

The shower responded with hot water immediately she turned it on and there were fresh towels on the shelves in the boat's little bathroom. After turning the shower off again, she met Zeke on the sundeck as he climbed back onto the boat.

'All sorted.' He glanced at her white dress, which was speckled with smudges of dirt and river water, and then at his once immaculate trousers. 'I feel like I did as a child when I was sent out with orders to keep clean before some social function or other and I messed up. I was so used to roaming free in wide-open spaces I always forgot Mum's orders.'

She smiled at him, her eyes soft. 'You've a good excuse for messing up this time. And there's plenty of hot water, by the way.'

'Great.'

Would he invite her to share the shower with him?

And then she answered herself immediately, Why ask the road you know? Zeke was determined to keep to the decision they'd made when they were seeing each other before, namely that their wedding night would be their first time together. And it had been at her instigation, she knew that, because of what she'd confided to him. But she wasn't sure any of that mattered now, not after everything that had happened in the last six months and especially, *especially* after today. And what if he decided to finish their relationship? What if he got tired of all the complications included in the package that was Melody Taylor?

She stepped up to him, putting her arms round his neck and then wrinkling her nose. 'You smell incredibly earthy.'

'River water actually; slightly different.' He grinned at her, curving his arms round her waist. 'You feeling better now?' he asked softly.

'Sort of.' It helped to be close like this with his body warm and solid in front of her. He could smell as high as a kite for all she cared as long as he was alive and breathing. 'I was so scared, Zeke.'

'I'm sorry, sweetheart.' He folded her into him so her cheek was resting against the top of his chest. His skin was warm, the dried mud and debris from the river giving it a sandy feel. She didn't think she had ever wanted him so much as she did at that moment.

She lifted her face and stared at him bravely. 'I could do with a shower too and afterwards we could make use of the double bed in the rear cabin.'

His body seemed to still although the expression on his face didn't change. 'The ultimate reward for the ancient mariner?' he murmured after an excruciatingly long moment.

'I mean it,' she said, refusing to be dismissed by the mocking, slightly teasing tone.

'If you do mean it it's for all the wrong reasons.'

Melody closed her eyes for a moment. When she opened them the hard face could have been carved in granite. 'How can you say that? You don't know what's in my mind.'

'Wrong.' His voice was slow and deliberate. 'It's my job to read minds and I'm damn good at it. I can tell when a witness is lying almost before they open their mouth and I can assimilate what makes them tick too. You were scared out there as anyone would be, but added to that there's a whole cartload of mixed emotions flying about in your head.'

She tried to draw away, stung by his coolness, but he wouldn't let her, holding her fast.

'We split because you got it wrong; emotion number one. You want to trust me but you can't; emotion number two. I frightened you out there—you thought I might not come up again; emotion number three. You love me but you're not sure how much, emotion number four—'

'No.' She interrupted him then, her eyes changing as anger lit a little fire in the grey depths. 'I *am* sure how much I love you. And cut the psychoanalysis. You're a lawyer, not a psychiatrist.'

'One necessitates the other.'

She looked at him squarely. 'I trust you, Zeke. All right?' Suddenly it was there, maybe it had been there for days and she hadn't recognised it, but now she knew it was true. Whatever her father had been, whatever he had put her mother through, didn't mean Zeke was the same. She and Zeke were themselves, their relationship was their own private world and nothing and no one should impinge on it. He was a man of integrity; he'd shown her that from the first day they had met and he was still showing her it. It was enough that he was himself.

He eyed her, his mouth curving in a smile that had cynicism at its root. 'You'd do anything for me right now, say anything, and if it was any other woman but you I'd take the offering and relish it.'

She actually stamped her foot at him. 'Don't be so pigheaded! I'm not a child. I do actually have the capability of thinking my actions through.'

'A week ago you still believed I could be engaged to you and conducting an affair with another woman. That's fact, Melody.' Now he did release her. 'What's changed your mind so fast?'

She stared at him. He wasn't going to believe her whatever she might say. The irony of it was almost laughable. He thought she was the obstacle to their love but in fact it was him. Because there was nothing left but blatant truth she spoke it without considering her words. 'If you are asking me whether I've decided to recognise my doubts and fears for what they were and deal with them, then the answer is yes,' she said, amazed her voice could sound so rational when she was on fire inside. 'But if you're asking me to explain nightmares, visions which you know in the cold light of day were in your head but not from which deep recess of your mind they sprang from, then I can't. All I know is that I was wrong before. I was still living in the nightmare. Now I've woken up.'

He stared at her, blinking rapidly before raking his hair back from his face. 'This isn't the right time,' he repeated. 'You've had too many emotional supports knocked out from under you today.'

She could have kicked him. 'You've got it all figured

out, haven't you, but doesn't it ever cross your mind you could be wrong?'

He flexed broad shoulders and there was a weariness to the action which told her the incident with the child had taken more out of him than he would care to admit. It produced such a rush of love she had to bite her lip, even before he admitted, 'More often than you'll ever know.'

'Then why can't we just go with the flow?'

For a moment she thought he was going to acquiesce. Then he took a deep breath, his voice quiet when he said, 'The only flow I'm going with in the next little while is the one under the shower. I'm sorry, Melody, but this is the wrong time and the wrong place. If you want a shower, fine. I'll wait till you're finished.'

She studied him intently. The amber eyes were very direct and the ring of conviction in his voice was absolute. She knew a moment of blazing anger. 'I think you're a self-satisfied, hard, pompous know-all,' she said furiously.

'Be that as it may,' he said, infuriatingly calm, 'that's the deal. Now, do you want a shower?'

She told him exactly what he could do with his shower. Zeke's eyebrows rose. 'I'd prefer to use it in the traditional way if you don't mind.'

'I hate you.'

'No, you don't.' He pulled her into him with a violence that suggested his air of cool control was only skin-deep, kissing her until she didn't know what day it was. Then he pushed her down into the galley, pointing at the bottle of champagne now swimming in cold water in the ice bucket. 'Drink a glass or two of that and unwind,' he said. 'And if there's any coffee hidden about this place I'd like mine hot and black when I've showered. OK?'

She nodded, making sure he knew it was sulkily. She

thought she saw the firm mouth twitch before he disappeared into the end cabin after grabbing a towel from the bathroom *en route*. She reached for the bottle of champagne and then stilled, hearing the clink of a belt buckle followed by the unmistakable whirr of his trouser zip.

Melody closed her eyes tight but it didn't stop the pictures forming on the screen of her mind. She'd seen him stripped down to shorts the previous summer on a hot day when they'd played tennis with some friends, and he had looked magnificent then. Now her wicked imagination took things a step further.

When she heard him exit the cabin it took all of her willpower to casually sip her drink, her glance directed out of the galley window. She would *not* ogle him like a lovesick idiot, she told herself tensely. His ego was big enough as it was without her adding to it.

'I couldn't trouble you to try and brush some of the dried dirt off these, could I?'

She turned at the sound of his voice. Big mistake. Giant. Huge. She swallowed hard but although her voice sounded perfectly normal she couldn't do anything about the fiery glow in her cheeks. 'Of course.' She took the trousers—which were now virtually dry—from him as he stood at the bathroom door, trying to ignore the acres of bare flesh in front of her. The towel was in place round the lower half of his torso admittedly, but the lean, tanned body was breathtakingly on show.

'Thanks.'

The rat was totally unconcerned, Melody thought furiously as he nodded with an easy smile before stepping into the bathroom and pulling the sliding door closed. Which wasn't fair. First of all he'd spurned her and now he flaunted himself in front of her. She really did hate him and she didn't care if they never made love. She could do perfectly well with or without Zeke Russell in her life.

By the time she was on the sundeck and had thoroughly vented her mortification on the hapless trousers, reason kicked in. Zeke had always been so very much at ease with his masculinity, he wouldn't think anything of stripping down to next to nothing, she admitted grudgingly. He wasn't being intentionally awkward. She sighed long and hard. It was her. She didn't know what had happened to her libido recently but if she could turn the darn thing off, she would.

But worse was to come.

With the trousers airing on the sundeck to get rid of the last trace of dampness, Melody went down to the galley to hunt for coffee in the well-stocked cupboard. She found a half-used jar almost immediately, and after switching on the kettle was spooning coffee into two mugs when the bathroom door opened.

'You've found some coffee? Great.'

To her horror Zeke strolled into the galley, the towel wrapped low round his hips and his powerfully muscled body smelling deliciously of something lemony. His wet hair was slicked back from his forehead and a five-o'clock shadow on the square chin added to the overall dynamite in front of her Melody smiled weakly. 'Nice shower?' Feeble but the best she could do.

'Never appreciated one more.' He nodded to the kettle. 'It's boiled.'

She knew it had boiled. It was a carbon copy of what was happening inside her. 'I'll…I'll get your trousers first; they're just airing—'

'Don't bother.' He smiled, the amber of his eyes more golden than usual. 'Let's take a coffee onto the sundeck and relax for a few minutes. I think we both deserve it.'

Relax? With him stark naked? Practically. Was he mad? 'Fine.' She could do this. This was not beyond her.

Once on the sundeck Zeke sat down with his legs resting on the lower portion of the front of the boat, taking a long pull at the hot coffee and then sighing in satisfaction. 'Hell, but I needed that.'

'How are you feeling?' she asked quietly, carefully sitting at the side of him in such a way that no part of their bodies came into contact.

'OK now.' He stretched lazily and Melody trembled on the brink of hyperventilating. 'Better than that poor little tyke, I bet. At least I didn't swallow half of the Thames.'

'He did look sorry for himself when they drove off.' She tried to direct her gaze anywhere but at the flagrant maleness next to her, but it didn't help. She might be looking at the flowers starring the riverbank but the screen of her mind was replaying broad shoulders and a hairy chest along with hard and powerful thighs.

'Thanks for seeing to the trousers.' He had turned to look at her and Melody knew she had to look back; it would seem churlish not to. She met his eyes, smiling her reply because words were not an option right at that moment. A little robin flew to the rail of the boat, perching there for a moment before flying higher into one of the branches overhanging the deck.

Overwhelmingly grateful for the diversion, Melody decided robins were her favourite birds as she followed the little thing's progress with her eyes. 'He must be used to being fed by people on boats to be so tame,' she said brightly, pretending not to notice that Zeke hadn't taken his eyes off her face.

'It wasn't a rejection of you. You do know that, don't you?'

His voice was soft and low, so low she could barely hear him. She sat silent, unable to speak, her gaze resolutely trained on the robin. It looked down quizzically at her, as if questioning the motive for her interest, before suddenly flying away. Right. That told her, then.

'And if you've begun to let down the barriers I'm ecstatic.'

She did look at him then. 'You don't sound ecstatic.'

He had the grace to look a little discomfited.

'And might I question who isn't trusting who now?' she added tightly.

He frowned. 'That's not fair.'

Oh, they were talking unfairness here now, were they? 'I thought you were such an advocate for the truth, the whole truth and nothing but the truth,' she said crisply. 'Or is that only when it applies to the rest of the world?'

His frown deepened as muscles in his jaw tightened. He was getting angry, she thought with a distinct feeling of satisfaction mixed with relief. She could cope with angry but not a half-naked, beguiling Zeke, besides which she was glad he was feeling put out, considering she felt so wretched.

'You're being totally unreasonable.'

'Well, of course I am,' she agreed sarcastically. 'When you come out with the home truths it's in the cause of honesty and righteousness. When I point out a few, I'm unreasonable or deluded or both.'

'You're too emotionally upset by all that's happened today to see things clearly,' he said coldly.

Will you please stop playing the lawyer?' She was shouting now but she didn't care. 'It's driving me insane! Just be a man for a change, can't you? An ordinary, human man who might make the odd mistake.'

She whirled round, the dress providing Zeke with a

glimpse of lacy white panties, and stormed off into the galley. He followed a second later, his face as black as thunder. 'You really do take the biscuit,' he ground out icily. 'Self-absorbed doesn't even begin to describe it.'

'Oh, really?' She faced him, hands on hips and her chin stuck out at such an angle it would have made Zeke smile in different circumstances. 'Well, I can do the name thing too, believe me, so don't push your luck.'

'What's got into you today?' There was a thread of very real amazement in the blazing rage.

'You mean besides me trying to explain how I feel and being treated like a five-year-old child?' she flashed back furiously.

'I have not treated you like a child.'

'Well, you haven't treated me like a woman either.' *What the hell do you want from me?'*

She had never seen Zeke lose his temper, not even when she had flung back his ring at him all those months ago, but she was seeing it now. His voice was angry, harsh, and he sounded like a man at the end of his tether. For a second she was frightened, not of him physically—she knew he would rather cut off both hands than raise them to a woman—but of the tiger she'd unleashed.

'I mean tell me, I'd really like to know,' he bit out, his eyes glittering dangerously. 'You say I don't treat you like a woman. Is this what you want?' He jerked her into his arms, his mouth taking hers with no finesse at all as he moulded her shape against his.

The kiss had been intended as a punishment for her words but almost from the first it was something else. It might have been the way Melody instantly responded to the feel of his lips crushing hers or the fact that the sexual tension which had been between them all day had reached fever pitch. Whatever, in a moment or two there was no thought of chastisement given or received, just two mouths fused together as though they would never part and two bodies seemingly merging into one.

Desire was in Zeke's fingertips as he ran his hands possessively over her trembling body and Melody, her arms wrapped round his neck in total surrender, gave in to the hunger of running her hands over the hard, broad shoulders before tangling her fingers in his hair. His tongue was playing an erotic game in the sweetness of her mouth, the thin towel leaving her in no doubt as to what she was doing to him. She felt she was melting, molten, her legs barely capable of holding her as they swayed together in the privacy of the little galley.

One of his hands was in the small of her back, urging her softness against the hard ridge of him, and the other covered her breast, the thin bodice of the dress not disguising the swollen, aching evidence of her own desire. Their passion was frenzied, needing fulfilment to appease the fire, and as Zeke drew her into the cabin and the soft double bed Melody went willingly.

Her hands slid down his back, pushing at the towel as her mouth returned his fierce and hungry kisses, and then suddenly she stopped, aware of the change in him a moment before the voice outside the boat registered. Zeke stood very still for a second more before putting her from him and securing the towel more firmly round his hips.

She stood exactly where he had left her, hearing him walk into the galley and stand on one of the three narrow steps leading up to the deck as he called an answer. She knew why he hadn't climbed fully on deck as she remembered the taut hardness of his arousal, and it struck her she ought to go and assist in the situation. But still she didn't move.

She heard enough to realise one of the couples had come to let them know the representative from the boatyard had collected the boat and that they were now continuing on, and then a few moments later there was the sound of chinking crockery and then the kettle boiling again. A minute or two after that Zeke appeared in the doorway, clothed now in his shirt and trousers but with bare feet. 'Coffee's ready,' he said flatly. 'The other was cold.'

She stared at him for a second before he turned and walked back into the galley, whereupon she followed him. Melody wished her heart wasn't beating so deafeningly in her ears and she just prayed the trembling deep inside wasn't visible to the naked eye. Apart from that she felt numb, unreal. *He hadn't come back to her.* She didn't know if she was relieved or disappointed. She just knew he hadn't come back.

Zeke handed her the coffee and instinctively she wrapped her fingers round the warm mug. Suddenly she was cold, icy cold. She glanced at him and met his eyes, and just for a second she thought she detected a glimmer of uncertainty in his face, then decided against it. What did Zeke have to be uncertain about? There was no doubt in her mind that he always had the upper hand in their relationship, and all that had happened in the last few minutes proved it.

'I don't want your first time to be on a cramped little boat,' he said, still in a monotone. 'OK?'

She said nothing, drinking the coffee and welcoming the strength it put into her leaden limbs.

'I'm sorry,' he continued, his voice hollow, empty. 'I shouldn't have let it get to the point it did. You have to be sure of what you're doing, Melody. Sure of what you feel and what you've decided. I don't want any regrets.'

'For you or me?' she asked woodenly.

'For both of us. I'm selfish enough to admit it's for both of us.'

Facing each other, they drank the coffee without further conversation. The silence throbbed with tension but for the life of her Melody couldn't break it or begin to act naturally. She felt shattered by all that had happened but she didn't want to analyse why right now. Not until she was alone. Ridiculous, but she felt she'd lost him and then found him, only to lose him again.

For the first time since they had started seeing each other again, she acknowledged their relationship had changed. It was different, subtly different from how it had been before the split. At first she had thought it was just that they needed to get used to each other again, make room for each other in their lives once more, but it was more than that. Quite what she couldn't put her finger on but it was something else she needed to think about when she was alone.

She glanced at her wrist-watch. It was nearly six o'clock. He was expecting that they would spend the evening together but she couldn't. She couldn't take his nearness, the magnetic pull of him, until she had sorted things out in her mind.

She swallowed hard. 'You're right,' she said raggedly. 'I *am* emotionally upset and it's tired me out. Could… could we go back now, please? I'd like to go to bed early if it's all right with you. I've a headache.' It was perfectly true—her head was pounding fit to burst.

'If that's what you want.' His face was inscrutable.

'It is.'

He nodded, putting his empty mug down and leaving the galley without further ado.

CHAPTER NINE

WHEN Melody awoke to the phone ringing at eight o'clock the next morning she felt as though she had the mother and father of a hangover, although it was exhaustion—not alcohol—which was making her head throb and inducing the feeling of nausea. When Zeke had dropped her off at the bedsit the night before she had walked the floor until the early hours, finally drifting off to sleep as the dawn had reached tentative fingers into her window.

Groaning, she rolled onto her back and sat up, reaching for the phone with sleep-clumsy fingers. Her mouth felt as dry as a bone. 'Melody Taylor,' she croaked wearily.

'Melody?' Her mother's voice was disgustingly bright. 'Why haven't you rung me? Did you get the messages I left on your answer machine yesterday?'

She hadn't even checked to see if there were any. 'No.' She gave no further explanation.

'Oh.' There was a little pause. 'Are you all right?'

'Migraine.' It wasn't actually and she shouldn't lie about it or else she might develop one as judgement on her, but her mother suffered with migraines and it was the one excuse that would suffice to prevent further conversation.

'Poor you,' her mother said a little abstractedly. 'You

won't want to come to Sunday lunch, then. I had some good news about the case yesterday and I was inviting you and Zeke to lunch to discuss it. He's already rung to say he's coming. He rang last night,' she added pointedly.

Bully for him. Melody glared at the receiver, acute disappointment at the thought of not seeing Zeke warring with the knowledge that she couldn't cope *with* seeing him. Not today. Not until she'd got her head round things. She'd fobbed him off last night by saying she wasn't feeling great and she'd ring to let him know how she felt in the morning after he had suggested lunch. 'I'm having the day in bed,' Melody said, keeping her voice low as befitted a migraine-sufferer. 'I've a busy day at work tomorrow and I must be OK for it. I was going to ring Zeke to tell him but perhaps you could do that for me?'

'Me?' asked her mother in surprise. 'Well, yes; yes, of course, if you want me to.'

'Thanks.' She had no wish to prolong this. 'Goodbye, Mother.' It was only after she had put the telephone down that Melody realised she hadn't asked her mother what the good news entailed. She'd lost a good few brownie points there, then.

She rolled over again, deciding she'd treat herself to the luxury of a bit of a lie-in, considering her awful night, but knowing full well thoughts of Zeke would crowd her head now she was awake. The next thing she knew it was midday and Caroline was banging on her door.

'Flipping heck, Mel. You must have had one blinding night with lover-boy to look like this,' was Caroline's cheerful greeting as she bounced into the bedsit.

Melody winced. All this exuberance was a little hard to take when she hadn't even had a cup of coffee. 'Not exactly,' she said flatly, shutting the door and walking over to her tiny kitchen area. 'I was just going to fix some coffee. Fancy one?'

'If there's a couple of slices of toast and jam to go with it.' Caroline grinned at her. She had decided to add black streaks to her spiky red hair a few days before and the result was somewhat disconcerting but strangely attractive. On Caroline anyway. 'So,' she continued, perching herself on the end of the bed as she watched Melody pull out the toaster. 'What gives? If the bags under your eyes aren't the result of a wild night of passion with Mr Zipper, what's happened?'

Melody filled her in on events—without going into details about the bedroom scene—and Caroline sat cross-legged and open-mouthed at the end of it. 'Do you mean to say—' Caroline's voice was incredulous '—that *he* was the one to stop?'

Melody frowned. Caroline needn't rub it in. 'Yes.'

'And he's never… You've never…'

'No. I mean, he *has*, with other women. Lots of other women,' she added as an afterthought. 'But right at the beginning of us dating I said I wanted to wait and so…' She shrugged.

'Wow.' Caroline stared at her. 'There aren't any more like him at home, are there? Not that I'd want him to wait, of course—in fact, I'd probably have his trousers off before you could say Jack Robinson—but the fact that he thinks enough of you to do that… Dreamy,' she finished with a little sigh. Then she frowned. 'But if you were the one who wanted to wait till you'd been holy-watered and incensed and all that, what's the problem?'

Melody set Caroline's toast and coffee on the little dining table before fetching her own, and it was only when they were both sitting down that she said, 'It's not as simple as that, not now. He doesn't believe that I trust him. He thinks…' She shook her head. 'I'm not sure what he thinks any more,' she finished miserably. 'Only that I don't love him enough or trust him.'

Caroline finished one slice of toast. 'You can't blame the guy,' she said very quietly.

n 'What?' Melody couldn't believe her ears. Caroline was always on her side, fiercely so.

Caroline wriggled uncomfortably at the look on Melody's face but stuck to her guns. 'Look at it from where he's standing, Mel,' she said, beginning to tick points off on her red-taloned fingers. 'The guy's a candidate for sainthood. Then you dump him on the strength of some trumped-up photos your mother's got hold of through a private detective. *A private detective*,' she emphasised as though Melody were hard of hearing. 'Six months later you swan back and after a brief skirmish it's all hearts and roses. He finds he's flavour of the month again. I mean—' she took a huge bite of toast, chewing and swallowing before she continued '—it's confusing if nothing else. Especially now you've changed from shrinking violet to carnivorous fly-catcher. Or man-catcher anyway.'

Her relationship with Zeke as seen through the eyes of Caroline. Melody didn't know if she wanted to laugh or cry. Instead she said, 'It's not like that.'

Caroline finished her toast, licking sticky fingers thoroughly. 'You don't accept you've sent some pretty mixed signals to the poor guy?' she asked softly, suddenly very serious.

Melody looked into the big blue eyes and saw only concern there. It enabled her to mutter, 'I don't know. Perhaps… Yes, I guess so.'

'But he's still hanging on in there?'

Not quite how she would have put it, but, 'Yes,' Melody said. 'Yes, I suppose he is.'

'Then—and excuse me if I've missed something here—why have *you* got the hump with *him*?'

Put like that, she didn't know. Melody gazed helplessly at her friend.

'Look, I know your mother didn't do you any favours by playing around with your mind from when you were a baby, but can't you give the guy a break? You say you trust him, so prove it. Trust he won't dump you while you wait for him to see you mean what you say. Stop insisting he has to believe what you say immediately and instead take time and show him. Just…chill out.' Caroline grinned at her. 'Savvy? He might come round quicker than you think.'

She got to her feet, leaving Melody still sitting at the table, deep in thought. 'I'm going to have a bath and then veg; I had a *heavy* date last night,' she proffered, walking across to the door and opening it before she added, 'And the price for all this wisdom and experience is that I want to be bridesmaid, OK? For some reason I've yet to work out, all my relations and friends balk at the thought of me as bridesmaid.'

Melody looked over at the pretty little face underneath the bright red and black spikes, the traces of last night's make-up giving the blue eyes a panda look, and smiled with genuine warmth. 'I can't think why,' she said softly. 'There's no one I'd like better to support me on such a big day. You can even pick the colour you want—as long as it's not black,' she added hurriedly. 'Course, you *do* realise this is all academic? Right at this moment he might be thinking he'd be better off cutting his losses and moving on to someone who isn't all screwed up.'

'Oops, where's the trust gone?' Caroline shook her head in admonishment. 'I think I hear echoes of dear Mother here. Now, say after me, I *will* trust Zeke and I am not screwed up.'

'I will trust Zeke and I am not screwed up.'

'Good girl. And repeat that at least one hundred times every day. And as for the little set-back yesterday—just tell him it's the pmt or something. Whenever I lose it I blame it on that. It's wonderful being a woman, isn't it?' she added wickedly, giggling as she closed the door behind her.

Melody's smile faded as she continued to stare across the room. She'd give the world to be like Caroline. And then as clearly as if someone had spoken out loud a little voice in her head said, But if you were, Zeke wouldn't love you because he's fallen in love with *you*. You. Not Caroline, not one of the other women he's known in the past. You.

She made herself another cup of coffee and round of toast, suddenly finding she was ravenous. She had some serious thinking to do today and she always thought better on a full stomach.

Of course their relationship was different this second time round, she told herself a little while later. She had panicked about that yesterday but she needn't. After all that had happened it couldn't be otherwise, but that didn't mean it had to be *worse* than before. That was her negativity kicking in again. It could be better; they could be closer with issues faced and dealt with. As Caroline had said, Zeke was hanging on in there. That had to mean something. It had to mean a *lot*.

Melody spent the rest of the day cleaning the bedsit, catching up with her washing and ironing and treating herself to a long, leisurely soak in the bath come evening.

She gave herself a manicure and pedicure, painting the nails on her hands and feet with some nail polish Caroline had given her for Christmas but which she'd never used. It was called Sexy Nights and was a rich dark red, quite different from the pastel shades she normally used. She was amazed how good it made her feel.

She was sitting in an immaculate bedsit, her hair newly washed and conditioned, every inch of skin on her body and face moisturised and with her nails blazing a statement, when the telephone rang at eight o'clock. She knew before she picked up the receiver it was Zeke.

'Hi.' His voice was warm and deep and Melody felt her spine tingle. 'How are you feeling?'

For a second she thought he meant about the happenings of the day before and then she remembered she was supposed to have a migraine. Oh, what a tangled web we weave, when we first practise to deceive, she thought wryly. 'Much better, thank you,' she said softly. 'You had lunch with Mum, then?'

'A very good lunch. She's an excellent cook.'

That was true, but she'd never thought to hear Zeke give any accolades in that direction.

'I had tea too. Crumpets with strawberry jam and some homemade fruit cake.'

Melody's eyes widened. Trying to keep the amazement out of her voice, she said, 'You stayed for tea? Did the business take that long?'

'No.' It was airy. 'That was settled fairly quickly. The other party is accepting an out-of-court one-off payment for loss of business et cetera, but better than that, they've agreed to carry on using your mother's firm, which is the main thing. If they'd pulled the plug word soon gets around about a supplier being unreliable, added to which they're your mother's main money-spinner. So, all's well that ends well.'

'Oh, Zeke, thank you.' Emotion bubbled and she tried to keep a lid on it. After the day before he must think she was a nutcase as it was. 'You don't know what this will mean to her.'

'I've a pretty good idea,' he said drily. 'She cried for about half an hour and then insisted I stay for the afternoon and tea. I had a job to get away even then.'

And they say miracles didn't happen. Melody took a deep breath and summoned up all her courage. 'I'm sorry about yesterday,' she said. 'It was all my fault. I just want to say one thing, though, in the cold light of day, as it were. I was wrong six months ago and it put us both through a whole lot of pain that needn't have happened, but perhaps in the long run something like that needed to occur. To...to wake me up. And I have—woken up, I mean. I hope you'll believe that one day. But for now maybe we both need to loosen up. Me especially,' she added with a touch of ruefulness.

There was silence and her heart began to thud uncomfortably hard. Had Caroline got it wrong? Had *she* got it wrong? Caroline had only had the situation presented to her from one point of view after all. If she'd led the other girl to think Zeke thought more of her than he did... She forced herself to keep quiet.

'I love you.' It was husky.

She was so glad she hadn't rushed in where angels feared to tread. 'I love you too,' she said, a little shakily.

'We'll work things out.'

'I know.' She wouldn't accept anything other than that.

'But—' a moment's pause '—I have to fly to the States tonight. I'm waiting for a taxi right now.'

But that was further away than Scotland. She pushed the ridiculous thought aside. 'How long for?' she managed at last. 'And what about the wedding on Saturday?'

'Well, fortunately we did Brad's stag weekend a month ago but that's a different story. Anyway, I have to be back by Thursday night because there's a hundred and one details to see to on Friday in my role as best man. But it'll be fine. No problem.'

'I'll miss you. First Scotland and now this.'

'Crazy, isn't it?' His voice was very soft. 'I haven't had a case that takes me away from London for months, and then it happens twice as soon as we start seeing each other. I'm sorry, sweetheart.'

'Luck of the draw.' She was pleased how matter-of-fact her voice sounded because disappointment that she hadn't seen him today was so strong she could taste it. 'You can't get out of it, I suppose?'

'No. Tricky case with a mass of complications and I've been dealing with it for months. I had a phone call when I was with your mother and they'd already reserved my seat on a plane that leaves Heathrow before midnight.'

'You'll call me? Even with the time difference?'

'Every night. Look, I'm going to have to go. I've got to call at the office and pick up some files on the way to the airport. I'm sorry, sweetheart. I'll try and phone a bit later.'

'OK.' She didn't want him to put down the phone. She *wished* she'd seen him today. She wished yesterday hadn't been such a wash-out. 'How are you feeling?' she asked quickly. 'After your swim in the Thames?'

'Fine.' She could tell he was relieved she'd taken the news of this sudden trip so well and it suddenly dawned on her Angela would no doubt be accompanying him. 'Bye, sweetheart,' he said softly. 'Be good.'

'You too; don't work too hard,' she said bravely.

As soon as she put down the telephone the idea came

to her. She would call a cab and meet him at the airport. Say goodbye properly, maybe even have a coffee with him if there was time before his flight. She didn't want to be brave—she wanted to *see* him. *What about Angela?* She closed her eyes tightly for a moment. She would have to wave them off together, smile brightly, do the confidence thing. Could she?

She owed him. She owed him this if nothing else. If she was going to start showing him she trusted him, as Caroline had suggested, it had to start now, today.

What if you get to the airport and they're…too friendly?

No. She opened her eyes, her mouth settling in a determined line. She wasn't going to listen to the gremlins. A secretary and her boss had to get on well for their working relationship to be successful, and Zeke would know where to draw the line in the sand.

But he's so attractive, that's the thing. He's always stood out from the crowd like a heartthrob of the silver screen. It appeared he had even talked her *mother* round, for goodness' sake. No other man could have done that.

Melody picked up the phone. He couldn't help how he looked any more than he could help that indefinable something that made him sheer dynamite. That was all to do with ancestry, genealogy, whatever. What he could help was the type of person he was—his ethics, moral code, principles—and he had never given her reason to doubt him. She thought he had but she had been mistaken.

The argument settled in her head, she called for a cab and then dashed about getting ready. Her hands stilled on the first pair of jeans that came to light. Zeke might not have designs on his secretary but it wouldn't hurt to show the other woman she was more than a match for her. Instead she pulled out a new pair that clung in all the right places, along with a little black short-sleeved cashmere top that just skimmed her waist.

Her hair was perfect—she blessed the fact she'd spent time on it that evening—and with a touch of light make-up she was ready just as the taxi drew up.

It was warm outside as she opened the front door of the house and ran to the taxi, the heat of the day evident still, but she had little goose-pimples flickering over her skin. She *was* doing the right thing, she reassured herself for the umpteenth time, and if Angela thought she was a little over-the top, possessive even, in turning up like this—well, that was all to the good in the long run. She narrowed her eyes at the view flashing past the window as the taxi gathered speed. The rules that were laid down without a word being spoken were always the most effective. She just hoped Zeke was pleased to see her. Please, please don't let this go wrong, she prayed silently all the way to the airport.

Melody arrived fifteen minutes or so before Zeke walked into the airport. She stood waiting close to the check-in for the flight. She saw him long before he saw her, her heart jumping as he walked in her direction, a slight frown wrinkling his brow and his mind obviously a million miles away from his surroundings.

As ever the throng parted for him—something he was completely unaware of but which happened whenever she was with him. Why was that? she asked herself for a millisecond, answering in the same instant, whatever it was, it was the same phenomenon that caused women to swoon—good, old-fashioned word, that, but so appropriate where Zeke was concerned—and men to consider it a privilege to be called his friend.

Oh, she loved him. She loved him so, so much.

She waited for the moment when he would notice her.

* * *

Zeke knew he was in a foul mood. He'd known it even before the taxi driver had taken umbrage at his clipped replies to the man's chatter, taking the hefty tip Zeke gave him by way of apology with a surly growl of thanks.

The thing was, he didn't *want* to go to the States, he told himself irritably. For the first time in his life he would have been more than prepared to see a case he had worked on— and given one hell of a lot of blood, sweat and tears to— passed over to someone else. Duffy could have gone, or even Cornwell at a pinch, but the client hadn't been prepared to be swayed. So here he was, set for America for several days with no chance of seeing Melody and determining how she was feeling about the travesty that was yesterday. *Damn it.*

He'd done everything wrong. As he began to walk across the terminal he was back on the boat with Melody, seeing her face, the look in her eyes, the way she had spoken. When she'd spoken about trusting him he'd been nothing short of crass, he knew that, but he hadn't been able to find the right words to express what he felt. Him. The high-flying lawyer who had a reputation for the silver tongue that could turn rapier-sharp when it had to. He earnt his living by knowing exactly what to say and when to say it or keep quiet. Why did all that fly out of the window when he was with her?

He groaned inside. The day had been disastrous, that was the truth of it, even before the incident with the child. Full of tension, hurt, every damn thing. What was he *doing*, for crying out loud?

She had told him again on the phone tonight that she had woken up to all that was wrong before, faced it, dealt with it. All he had to do was to accept it. So what was the matter with him? What was stopping him asking her to marry him again?

Cowardice. A voice in his head provided the answer with the type of cold-blooded ruthlessness he used in the courtroom. He was scared stiff of believing her and then being let down again because in spite of all his fine words he didn't think he could go there again, not without it breaking him. And Zeke Russell couldn't be broken, could he, not the big man, the hard, merciless lawyer who went for the jugular every time and came out on top?

She was his Achilles heel. She sure as hell wouldn't be flattered by the description, but that was what she was. With Melody he became vulnerable just like the next man and it scared him to death. He hadn't fully realised her power over him until she had left him and then he felt as though he'd been hit with an emotional sledgehammer. And even now she was throwing him off balance in every damn way possible, just as she'd been doing since their first encounter.

But he couldn't do without her. His eyes narrowed as he approached the check-in. And all this talk about waiting until she was sure she could trust him and the rest of it— he couldn't keep it up. Yesterday had proved that. He'd damn near taken her in that creaking little bed on a boat on the river where any Tom, Dick or Harry could have interrupted them. What had he been thinking of? But he hadn't been thinking, that was the thing. Not with the scent and feel of her in his eyes, his nostrils, under his hands. He'd wanted to eat her alive.

'Zeke?'

Such had been the nature of his thoughts that when he heard the quiet voice just behind him he ignored it for a moment, thinking it was in his head. But when it came again he turned. And there she was. In front of him. Everything he had ever wanted and would want for the rest of his life.

'I had to come. You don't mind?' she said, nervousness in her fluttering hands but love in her face.

He dropped his case and briefcase, giving a choked laugh as he drew her into his arms and then held her as if he would never let her go. 'Mind?' he whispered into the soft skin of her neck. 'What are you talking about? Don't you realise you are my world, my existence? How could I mind you being here?'

He kissed her, crushing her lips under his, his hunger so profound and intense he gave no thought to their surroundings. And Melody kissed him back, straining into him as though she would merge with his flesh.

How long they stood there like that neither of them knew, but eventually their emotions descended to a more controllable plane and they drew apart slightly, shaken but unwilling to let each other go even for a second.

Melody gazed into his dear, dear face and knew the time of holding back, of self-preservation had long since gone. He had her mind and her heart and her soul; she was utterly defenceless and unprotected but it didn't matter now because he had said she was his world and she believed him. 'I love you so much,' she whispered. 'I just had to come and tell you before you left. I know it's only for a few days but it will seem like a lifetime, knowing you're so far away.'

'And I love you, my darling; I have from the first time I saw you. It hit me like a bolt of lightning between the eyes and I haven't been the same since. Ask Brad or any of my friends,' he added ruefully. He kissed her again, touching her face with a gentle hand. 'There could never be anyone else for me. Do you believe that?'

She nodded wordlessly, unable to speak.

'Really, truly believe it?'

She nodded again, finding the words to reassure him. 'With all my heart.'

'Melody, I never planned to do this in a public place with people milling about,' he said a trifle desperately. 'I wanted it to be like last time—a candlelit dinner, roses on the table, the ring all ready to present, but I have to say it. Will you marry me? Soon, very soon?'

She had no trouble finding the words now. 'Yes, please,' she said immediately, 'and this *is* the perfect place.'

'It is?'

'Oh, yes. You're here and that makes it perfect.' She wrapped her arms tightly round his neck.

This time his kiss was long and lingering, and when he finally raised his head it was with a deep sigh. 'I wish I didn't have to go,' he said huskily. 'The timing's lousy.'

'You don't have to leave this minute?' she said anxiously.

He hugged her to him, bringing her into a protective embrace nestled under his chin. 'Of course not. Look, let me check in and then we'll find somewhere to sit and talk, have a coffee, yes?'

Melody nodded, and then spoke very steadily when she said, 'What about Angela? Have you arranged to meet her anywhere specific or just in Departures?'

'Angela?' His brow wrinkled and then cleared. 'Oh, Angela. She's not coming with me this trip. I worried about her flying when we went to Scotland, although she was perfectly happy to go, but the States is a different kettle of fish. A secretary will be provided for me out there if I need one. It's not a problem.'

'Right.' She stared at him. She was missing something here. Why on earth would he worry about Angela flying?

'I'll be back in a moment.'

He walked off to the check-in desk before she could ask him but she couldn't deny the feeling of relief that Angela wasn't travelling with him. She had never experienced the little green-eyed monster of jealousy before she'd met Zeke, but then she'd never been in love before, she excused herself guiltily.

It couldn't have been ten seconds later when the woman in question walked past her, taking her so by surprise all Melody could do was to stare as Angela approached Zeke, tapping him on the shoulder. She was too far away to hear what was being said but she saw Angela proffer what looked like a plastic folder full of papers as Zeke turned to face her.

Melody's heart began to pound. She hadn't really noticed Angela until the other woman had passed her, but from the back the secretary looked good, too good for approaching ten o'clock on a Sunday night. If she hadn't dressed up especially for Zeke, why was Angela's hair so perfectly coiffeured and why the elegant, floaty dress and dressy sandals?

Stop it, she warned herself silently. The other woman was entitled to wear whatever she wanted; not everyone relaxed or put their feet up on a Sunday evening in preparation for the week ahead. Besides, it didn't matter how Angela viewed Zeke—only how he viewed his secretary. Women were always going to fancy the pants off him, she knew that. Nevertheless, she couldn't take her eyes off them.

She saw Zeke say something and then smile, gesturing towards her before raising his hand in acknowledgement of her stare. She forced herself to smile back, and then as they both began to walk towards her she saw something that might go some way to explaining the floaty dress. Angela was pregnant, obviously so, she realised as they reached her.

'Melody, I don't think you've met my secretary?' Zeke said formally as he slid his arm round her waist before glancing at Angela. 'Angela, this is my fiancée.'

'Fiancée?' The other woman's carefully made-up eyes widened but she recovered her poise immediately, having the good taste not to ask questions but just to say, 'I'm pleased to meet you, Melody.'

'I'm pleased to meet you too,' Melody lied.

'After I'd phoned Angela earlier to let her know I was leaving for the States she remembered she'd taken one of the folders I might need out of the appropriate file to work on.' Zeke lifted the zipped plastic folder in his hand.

'I tried to catch him at home and then the office but he must have left,' Angela said, 'so I got my hubby to drive me to the office to collect it and then here.' She smiled a perfect white smile at Melody. 'He's waiting for me, so I must dash.'

'Thanks for this.' Zeke nodded to the folder.

'My pleasure.' Angela dimpled at him. 'We'd got Simon's parents round so it was a good excuse to bundle them off.' She turned to Melody and said by way of explanation, 'They live in Spain and are over here for a fleeting visit to see Simon's sister, who's just delivered their first grandchild. They didn't expect this—' she pointed to her rounded stomach '—considering we've only been married two months. We thought we could get away with telling them when I had it, *fait accompli* and all that, but the best-laid plans of mice and men... They're a bit strait-laced, you see. Nice, but strait-laced.'

Melody was feeling a little shell-shocked. She had the feeling Angela and Caroline would get on very well. 'When is the baby due?' she asked politely.

'First week of October.' Angela wrinkled her beautiful

little nose. 'Didn't plan that very well, did we, with the winter and all? Mind, we didn't plan it at all, as you've probably guessed.' She gave a Caroline-type giggle.

A tall, dark and extremely good-looking airline pilot walked past and Angela's gaze followed him for a second.

'Anyway,' she continued once she'd dragged her eyes back to Melody, 'we're thrilled about it now and I can't wait to be a mum, although I feel bad about letting Zeke down. Simon wants to bring the baby up away from the city fumes, so we're moving to the country. All wellingtons and mud and manure,' she added disconsolately, her gaze wandering again as a Richard Gere look-alike in a smart business suit passed by. 'Must go anyway. Bye.'

She could be wrong, Melody thought as she watched Angela totter away on the high heels, but she had the feeling Simon thought he had more chance of staying Angela's husband if she was buried in the country with a child to boot. She didn't say this to Zeke though, merely commenting, 'You didn't say Angela was having a baby.'

He looked at her in surprise. 'Is it important?'

For such an astute man he could be very dense at times. Melody smiled. 'No, it's not important at all.'

'Damn it, the most I can offer you is a coffee with a million other people around,' Zeke said, 'when what I really want to do is to go somewhere very private and shut the rest of the world out.'

Angela dismissed out of court. It felt extremely good. 'What would you say to me if we were somewhere very private?' she asked as they began to walk.

'What I was thinking of didn't involve conversation.' He pulled her closer against him. 'So maybe it's as well I've got a few days to cool down and regain control.'

'Zeke Russell in danger of losing control? Never.'

'Oh, lady, you've no idea.'

Zeke brought two lattes and sticky buns to the little table in the most secluded part of the coffee shop, but neither of them touched anything except each other. Their fingers linked, they gazed into each other's eyes and murmured words of love until it became imperative for Zeke to leave.

Melody walked with him as far as she could, determined she wasn't going to send him off with the memory of her in tears to cheer him throughout the flight to America. She managed really well until he took her into his arms, careless of onlookers, and crushed her to him. All the agony and need of the last six months was in his embrace and it melted her. She started to cry, holding on to him as though her life depended on it.

'I'll be back in a few days and after Brad's wedding we'll discuss ours, OK? Why don't you look for that white dress while I'm gone?' His voice was husky and she forced herself to let him go, drawing back a little but still within the circle of his arms as she stared up at him, her mouth soft and vulnerable. 'Are you game for a special licence?' he asked shakily. 'I know a guy who manages a big hotel and his speciality is candyfloss weddings. He'll pull out all the stops and make it beautiful. If I let him know what we want he'll provide the minister and everything else.'

'I only want you,' she whispered, her eyes luminous.

He smiled, drawing her against him again with one hand in the small of her back and the other cradling her head and stroking her hair. She felt a deep shudder shake him as he pressed his lips against the silk of her hair. 'I want this to be as you've always imagined it,' he murmured thickly. 'We've got the rest of our lives in front of us to enjoy each other and I intend to enjoy you, make no mistake about that.'

'One lifetime won't be enough.'

'Then I'll make sure we have two, three, however many you want,' he promised passionately, kissing her one last time.

'A million?'

'A million it is.'

By the time Zeke passed through into the departure area a few minutes later Melody was able to send him off with the memory of her smiling, even if it was a little tremulously.

CHAPTER TEN

MELODY lived only for Zeke's phone calls over the next few days. She still functioned at work, dealing with patients and their families with her usual gentle efficiency, a little part of her amazed that no one detected she was working on automatic. But they didn't. Which only proved she was a far better actress than she'd imagined, she told herself wryly.

When she told her mother about Zeke's proposal and the prospect of a very early wedding, Anna was quietly supportive. Which was amazing, positively amazing.

When she told Caroline the roof nearly went off the house, which wasn't surprising at all.

'I knew it!' Caroline did a kind of victory dance round the bedsit before dropping, exhausted, onto the sofa. 'I just knew it. You lightened up, didn't you? Let him do all the running? They love it, the macho guys. It's the me Tarzan, you Jane thing. Works every time.'

Melody didn't have the heart to tell her she'd raced to the airport and buttonholed him before he'd stepped on the plane. Instead she said, 'You being bridesmaid? From the way Zeke was talking we've got weeks rather than months to find our dresses, if not days. Have you got any lunch hours free this week?'

'Every one,' said Caroline immediately, adding, with a vulnerability that touched Melody, 'but you don't have to have me as bridesmaid. I know I'm not the traditional pale-lemon and flowers-in-the-hair type and I wouldn't want to spoil your photos and everything. As long as I can see you get married that'll be enough for me.'

'Well, it won't for me,' Melody declared firmly. 'I want you as bridesmaid and I've never liked pale lemon anyway.'

By the time Melody met Zeke off the plane on Thursday evening she had her fairy-tale dress, and Caroline had— if not your classic A-line creation—something both girls were happy with.

After their broken phrases of love, punctuated with kisses and caresses moderated a little, Melody told Zeke she'd asked Caroline to be her bridesmaid. She knew exactly why she loved him so much when he didn't even blink before he said, 'Great. That's great, honey. You'd better tell her to keep herself available for two weeks today, then.'

'Two weeks?' In spite of her knowing Zeke never hesitated once he'd made up his mind about something, Melody's voice was a squeak. 'That soon?'

'You bet.' His eyes devoured her. 'Brad gets back from Venice a day or so before, so he's doing the honours as best man. The hotel's booked along with the minister they use; the flowers, cake, cars are seen to and so is all the necessary red tape.'

'You *have* been busy.'

'Not me—Angela. She's had a whale of a time organising everything and throwing my money around.' He grinned at her. 'But the honeymoon I'm seeing to, OK? As a surprise. All you have to do now is to draw up a list of people you want to come along with telephone numbers, and Angela will take care of that too over the weekend.'

Melody was feeling hugely guilty at ever viewing Zeke's secretary as less than ideal. 'I can't believe everything's been arranged so fast,' she said a little dazedly.

'Helps it's not a weekend,' Zeke said practically as they began to walk out of the airport. 'You won't have any problem with your work?'

Melody shook her head, feeling giddy with love as he pressed her into his side with his free arm round her waist, the other holding his case with his briefcase tucked under his arm. 'I've worked so many extra hours in the last six months I'm overdue a huge amount of leave, besides which they've just managed to recruit two more therapists for the department, so it couldn't have worked out better.'

She didn't add that when she'd explained the circumstances and that she might be getting married very soon, the news had spread like wildfire on the hospital grapevine. The last few days had been ones of countless congratulations and oohing and ahhing. Everyone seemed tickled pink.

They spent the rest of the evening wrapped in each other's arms after Melody had cooked a cosy meal and they'd opened a bottle of wine, but even so it was hard to part when the taxi Zeke had called arrived. 'In two weeks' time we'll never have to say goodbye again,' Zeke whispered as he kissed her goodnight. 'Just keep thinking about that. And that I love you. More than life itself.'

'Not as much as I love you.'

'A hundred times more.'

He held her close to him for a moment and she inhaled the wonderful masculine smell of him, the scent of his aftershave combined with something that was all Zeke and intoxicating. She was the luckiest woman alive and she knew it.

* * *

The next two weeks flew by in such a whirl that Melody didn't know where she was most of the time. Brad and Kate's wedding day came and went and was voted a great success by everyone—especially Muffin, who stole the show in her little lace coat.

Melody went shopping with her mother at Anna's request—another first. They came home with the most extravagant, elegant mother-of-the-bride outfit in all of London.

The soft, flowing sleeveless dress with matching jacket in raw silk was a delicate shade of pale blue, the hat a marvellous concoction of silk and feathers and ribbons in exactly the same colour. Flushed and excited, Anna looked like a young girl buying her first grown-up dress in the shop mirror, her new tranquillity and joy in life—which was growing steadily with her visits to the therapist—reflected in her lovely face.

Zeke's widower uncle was part of the contingent coming over from America for the wedding, and he had agreed to give Melody away, which meant Anna was partnering him for the nuptials. She was incredibly nervous about this but once she had her outfit Melody detected a new confidence.

Melody and Caroline shopped for the bride's trousseau, Caroline stating that the new sexy underwear and transparent nightie and negligee were guaranteed to send Zeke crazy. Melody fingered the diaphanous material dreamily and just smiled.

And then, after a hundred tiny panics and blips—most of which were dealt with by a super-efficient Angela, who really was as good at her job as Zeke had declared—Melody awoke to a perfect wedding day of soft June sunshine and deep blue sky.

It had been decided she would get married from her old

home—mainly because she knew her mother would secretly like it—and so she and Caroline had slept the night there. Melody glanced over at the other girl, who was still sleeping soundly, spikes of red and black incongruous on Anna's lavender-scented fine lace pillowcases. Tonight she would be a married woman. Tonight there would be no more waiting, no more separations. She would be Zeke's and he would be hers.

Her heart began to thud and she glanced at her tiny alarm clock. Six o'clock. Far too early to wake everyone up—the wedding wasn't until twelve—but she couldn't stay in bed a second longer. She threw back the covers, padding across to the open window and kneeling so the heady perfume of the rambling roses climbing the wall below filled her senses.

She could trust him. She was doing the right thing and she could trust him. He loved her. He wouldn't break her heart the way her father had her mother's. She found she was telling herself the same thing over and over, nerves such as she hadn't experienced in the last two weeks rearing their ugly heads. But would she satisfy him? Be enough for him?

She wished she could speak to him, just hear his voice for a moment. Rising from her knees, she quietly felt for her mobile phone in her handbag, pulling on her bathrobe and slipping her feet into her fluffy slippers before she left the room.

Once in the garden she made her way to the old bench at the side of the house, finding it was already warm from the early heat of the sun. The birds were trilling in the trees overhanging the garden, fat honeybees buzzing in the roses and flowerbeds. Everything was peaceful, serene even, so why didn't she feel like that inside?

She gave herself a little shake. Stop it, she told herself

silently. This is just the old gremlins having one last try to spoil things. Don't let them. This is your wedding day; you're supposed to be radiant and eager and excited. And she was—partly. The other part of her felt choked by the pounding of her heart as fear flowed hot and strong. Fear that she wasn't good enough to hold the love of a man like Zeke, not forever. Things changed, emotions changed, men changed…

She couldn't ring him. She looked down at the phone in her hand, her throat constricting. She had spent the last two weeks adamantly declaring that she trusted him implicitly and it wasn't a lie. But… She rocked back and forth a few times, her hair feathering about her face and shoulders. No. She couldn't ring him. She placed the phone on the bench beside her. She mustn't.

When it warbled the silly little tune she'd chosen the second after her hand had let go, she wondered for a moment if she'd inadvertently activated a number. She snatched it up before reason asserted itself. Someone was ringing *her*. 'Hello?' she said tentatively, her voice a little shaky.

'Have I woken you up?'

'Zeke?' The relief, the wonder of hearing his deep, rich voice was almost too much. Calling on all her resources, she managed to continue, 'No, I'm awake. I'm sitting in the garden.'

'All by yourself?'

'Uh-huh. I…I couldn't sleep.'

'Nor could I,' he said, very softly. 'I need to tell you how much I love you, how I've always loved you and always will. Forever and beyond. And…to ask your forgiveness.'

'Forgiveness?' Her brow wrinkled.

'For asking too much of you too soon. Darling, I don't

expect there won't be times when the old doubts rear up and attack. It'd be impossible for them not to, simply because you *do* love me. I understand that, truly. All I ask is that at those times you don't keep it to yourself or try and muddle through. I want you to talk to me, to tell me how you're feeling so we can fight it together. If it's once a day or a hundred times a day, I don't care. But don't shut me out. I can't help you then. I can't protect you from yourself.'

She kept perfectly still, not breathing, not moving a muscle. He knew. Somehow he knew.

And then he confirmed it when he said, 'So, my beautiful soon-to-be wife, talk to me. Let me reassure you. Let me tell you you're the most sexy, amazing, beautiful woman I've ever seen, ever will see. The only woman I could envisage being my wife, the mother of my children. Talk to me and the fear will go, I promise. And one day in the future you will realise you haven't felt scared and panicky and lost since you can't remember when. And then you'll know you've been set free.'

'How did you know how I was feeling?' she whispered shakily.

'Because you're the other part of me.' And then his voice was very gruff when he said, 'You're not the only one to have fears, sweetheart. One of my living nightmares is replaying the moment you walked out of my life. I stood there, unable to move or speak and knowing I couldn't stop you.'

'Oh, Zeke.' She was crying now. Quite why she didn't know, but she'd never imagined him feeling scared of losing her. He was so confident, so assured, so aggressively male. 'I could never do that again. It nearly killed me the first time.'

'Likewise,' he said wryly, his voice sounding more

normal. 'So, no more creeping to somewhere quiet by yourself to try and sort your head out like this morning?'

'You weren't here this morning,' she pointed out softly.

'But I will be every morning for the rest of our lives,' he promised. 'I love you. I'm going to spend the rest of my life proving just how much starting tonight. In a few hours you'll belong to me in every sense of the word.'

'I know.' She shivered in the morning sunlight but it was with delicious anticipation, all her doubts dispelled.

'Mrs Russell.' His voice was a smoky caress. 'Sounds good, doesn't it?'

'Perfect.'

'Like you.' She could tell he was smiling now. 'My own sweet love. Now, go and start pampering yourself with hot oils and perfumes and whatever else you women do to make yourselves irresistible to us poor men.'

'Poor men my foot.' She was laughing. 'There's nothing poor about you, Zeke Russell.'

'Not when I've got you beside me. See you later, sweetheart. Don't keep us waiting too long, OK? My heart has taken enough of a battering as it is.'

'I'll be there on time, regardless of tradition.'

'I love you.' His voice trickled over her like warm honey.

'And I love you too.'

She was just about to press the button when he said, 'You still there, Melody?'

'Yes.'

'Just a thought to ponder on, but mum's the word in more ways than one. My uncle was very impressed with your mother last night.'

'He was?' Zeke and his uncle—a tall, broad Texan with

a craggy, tanned face and engaging smile—had come to the house for dinner with the three women the night before.

'Yeah. And he's not a man whose interest is stirred easily. My aunt died over five years ago now and, although plenty of women have made it plain they're willing to step into her shoes, he hasn't so much as had one date. And I could be wrong—' his tone made it clear he didn't think he ever was '—but I noticed a distinct gleam in your mother's eyes too. What do you think?'

She stared at a thrush having his morning wash and brush-up in her mother's birdbath in a corner of the garden. Come to think of it, her mother *had* been unusually animated last night, even girlish. She smiled slowly. 'Oh, Zeke. That would be wonderful, wouldn't it?'

'Early days,' he cautioned softly, 'but I've got a good feeling about this.'

'You haven't got a dishy relation for Caroline too?'

'Bit more of a challenge. I'll work on it.'

If Zeke was working on it Caroline was absolutely guaranteed a Texan hunk.

The marriage ceremony was being held in the grounds of the hotel, the chairs and rostrum decorated with the same ribbons and rose-scented posies as garlanded the massive reception room, where tables and chairs for two hundred guests were waiting. A long natural arch of willow in which a thousand pale cream and dusky-pink roses were entwined led the way to the platform to the side of which Zeke and Brad were sitting. Rows of six-foot flower displays provided an outer wall that encircled the whole area. It was a spectacle of scent and colour, and with the blue sky above and green grass below the perfect fairy-tale wedding. Then the music began.

Zeke turned to look at his bride as she was led to him on the arm of his uncle, and no one seeing his face could have doubted that this was a marriage made in heaven.

Melody was wearing a long, full gown of the palest rose-pink, the shade almost cream, with tiny crystals trimming the bodice and the edge of her veil. She carried a delicate bouquet of baby's breath and tiny pink and cream rosebuds and Zeke thought she seemed to float as she came towards him. He didn't even notice Caroline walking behind, her hair vying with the scarlet of her dress and a smile as wide as London Bridge splitting her face. Zeke had eyes for no one but his bride—and his bride for him— which was just as it should be.

After the short but beautiful ceremony champagne and strawberries were served to all the guests as the photographs were taken. It was a time of fun and laughter beneath a blazing June sky, and then they all trooped into the huge garden room overlooking the grounds where the ceremony had been held for a long, leisurely lunch. Later the tables were cleared for dancing and the French doors in the alcoves folded back so that guests could spill out onto the big patio beyond and sit under a starry sky.

And when the evening barbecue ended and Zeke and Melody made their farewells and disappeared to the extravagant bridal suite, he took her into his arms and kissed her until she had no breath left. They undressed each other slowly, savouring every moment as they tasted and nibbled and caressed until the hunger of their need was overwhelming. But still Zeke took his time.

'This is going to be perfect for you, Mrs Russell.'

His soft, possessive smile filled her with a sexy warmth as he drew her towards the enormous four-poster bed that dominated the room, and then he began to show her what true love between a man and woman was all about. Sexual feeling as hot and smooth as a river of perfumed oil began to flow through her as his hands and tongue worked their magic in her most intimate places, any shyness she'd felt at first burnt up in the flood of desire he was igniting.

His loving was bewitching, enchanting, and Melody responded with all the love in her heart, meeting him kiss for kiss and embrace for embrace, her boldness possible because of his passionate devotion to pleasing her. It seemed impossible so much feeling, so much emotion could be contained in her body without her melting.

By the time he levered his body over hers she was moist and ready for him, the brief moment of pain forgotten in the aching need inside her. And still Zeke controlled his own desire, building Melody's in intensity until he took them both into a realm of rapture that shook them to their very foundations.

Afterwards, as they lay sated in each other's arms, his hands wandering softly and soothingly over the fine silk of her skin, he told her of their honeymoon, his voice smoky and deep.

'A month in our own little hideaway high in the Blue Mountains in Jamaica,' he said, turning her to face him and stroking the wisps of hair from her cheeks with gentle fingers. 'It's a beautiful, rambling old white house with gardens ablaze with flowers and blossom trees and its own pool; my uncle bought it years ago when his wife was alive. They found they couldn't have children and so they followed another dream and escaped to their island idyll whenever they could. I only went there once with my parents many years ago when I was a boy, but it has always stayed in my mind as the most perfect spot in the world.'

'And your uncle doesn't mind us going?'

'He offered it as soon as he heard we were getting married,' said Zeke. 'I think he looks on me as the son he never had. We've always been close but we got closer after my parents were killed. It was a bad time and he was there for me one hundred per cent.'

The shadow that had darkened the tawny eyes lifted as he smiled. 'What's the betting your mother is going to see the place before the year's out?'

'You really think so?' Melody murmured, touching his handsome face as she spoke and secretly marvelling that they were together like this at last, with no more barriers between them—emotionally, mentally or physically.

'The way they were today I don't doubt it.' His smile widened. 'It'll cause a few complications, though—your mother and my mother-in-law becoming our aunt.'

Melody giggled, her hands beginning to stroke over the hard-muscled chest. 'I don't care,' she breathed softly, her fingers tangling in the wiry curls before she followed the line of hair past his navel and into the cradle for his manhood. As she touched him she felt him leap for her, renewed passion making his eyes glitter. 'I don't care about anything except you.'

'And I you, my sweet love. I'm going to make you happier and more fulfilled than any woman since the beginning of time.' And then he set out to prove he was a man of his word.

HARLEQUIN *Presents*

Harlequin Presents brings you
a brand-new duet by star author

Sharon Kendrick

THE GREEK BILLIONAIRES' BRIDES

Possessed by two Greek billionaire brothers

Alexandros Pavlidis always ended his affairs before
boredom struck. After a passionate relationship with
Rebecca Gibbs, he never expected to see her again.
Until she arrived at his office—pregnant, with twins!

Don't miss

THE GREEK TYCOON'S CONVENIENT WIFE,

on sale July 2008

www.eHarlequin.com

HP12744

Lucy Monroe

*delivers two more books from
her irresistible Royal Brides series.*

Billionaire businessman Sebastian Hawk and
Sheikh Amir are bound by one woman: Princess Lina.
Sebastian has been hired to protect Lina—but all he
wants to do is make her his. Amir has arranged to marry
her—but it's his virgin secretary he wants in his bed!

Two men driven by desire—who will they
make their brides?

FORBIDDEN: THE BILLIONAIRE'S VIRGIN PRINCESS

Sebastian Hawk is strong, passionate
and will do anything to claim the woman
he wants. Only, Lina is forbidden to him
and promised to another man....

Available July 2008

Don't miss
HIRED: THE SHEIKH'S SECRETARY MISTRESS
On sale August 2008
www.eHarlequin.com

HP12739

HARLEQUIN *Presents*

THE SICILIANS

They seek passion—at any price!

A sizzling trilogy by

Carole Mortimer

Two brothers and their cousin are all of
Sicilian birth—and all have revenge in mind
and romance in their destinies!

THE SICILIAN'S RUTHLESS MARRIAGE REVENGE

Sicilian billionaire Cesare Gambrelli blames the Ingram
dynasty for the death of his beloved sister. The beautiful
daughter of the Ingram family, Robin, is now the object
of his revenge by seduction....

On sale July 2008

Don't miss

AT THE SICILIAN'S
COUNT'S COMMAND

On sale August 2008

www.eHarlequin.com

HPI2742

REQUEST YOUR FREE BOOKS!

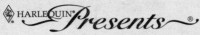

2 FREE NOVELS PLUS 2 FREE GIFTS!

YES! Please send me 2 FREE Harlequin Presents® novels and my 2 FREE gifts (gifts are worth about $10). After receiving them, if I don't wish to receive any more books, I can return the shipping statement marked "cancel". If I don't cancel, I will receive 6 brand-new novels every month and be billed just $4.05 per book in the U.S. or $4.74 per book in Canada, plus 25¢ shipping and handling per book and applicable taxes, if any*. That's a savings of close to 15% off the cover price! I understand that accepting the 2 free books and gifts places me under no obligation to buy anything. I can always return a shipment and cancel at any time. Even if I never buy another book, the two free books and gifts are mine to keep forever.

106 HDN ERRW 306 HDN ERRL

Name	(PLEASE PRINT)
Address	Apt. #
City	State/Prov.	Zip/Postal Code

Signature (if under 18, a parent or guardian must sign)

Mail to the Harlequin Reader Service:
IN U.S.A.: P.O. Box 1867, Buffalo, NY 14240-1867
IN CANADA: P.O. Box 609, Fort Erie, Ontario L2A 5X3

Not valid to current subscribers of Harlequin Presents books.

Want to try two free books from another line?
Call 1-800-873-8635 or visit www.morefreebooks.com.

* Terms and prices subject to change without notice. N.Y. residents add applicable sales tax. Canadian residents will be charged applicable provincial taxes and GST. Offer not valid in Quebec. This offer is limited to one order per household. All orders subject to approval. Credit or debit balances in a customer's account(s) may be offset by any other outstanding balance owed by or to the customer. Please allow 4 to 6 weeks for delivery. Offer available while quantities last.

Your Privacy: Harlequin Books is committed to protecting your privacy. Our Privacy Policy is available online at www.eHarlequin.com or upon request from the Reader Service. From time to time we make our lists of customers available to reputable third parties who may have a product or service of interest to you. If you would prefer we not share your name and address, please check here. ☐

HP08R

THE BOSS'S MISTRESS

Out of the office…and into his bed

These ruthless, powerful men are used
to having their own way in the office—
and with their mistresses they're also
boss in the bedroom!

**Don't miss any of our fantastic stories
in the July 2008 collection:**

#13 THE ITALIAN
TYCOON'S MISTRESS
by CATHY WILLIAMS

#14 RUTHLESS BOSS, HIRED WIFE
by KATE HEWITT

#15 IN THE TYCOON'S BED
by KATHRYN ROSS

#16 THE RICH MAN'S
RELUCTANT MISTRESS
by MARGARET MAYO

www.eHarlequin.com

HPE0708

Silhouette®

SPECIAL EDITION™

NEW YORK TIMES BESTSELLING AUTHOR

DIANA PALMER

A brand-new Long, Tall Texans novel

HEART OF STONE

Feeling unwanted and unloved, Keely returns
to Jacobsville and to Boone Sinclair, a rancher
troubled by his own past. Boone has always
seemed reserved, but now Keely discovers a
sensuality with him that quickly turns to love. Can
they each see past their own scars to let love in?

*Available September 2008
wherever you buy books.*

Visit Silhouette Books at www.eHarlequin.com   SSE24921